I0540937

THE
RELUCTANT GROOM
BRIDES OF SEATTLE SERIES

KIMBERLY ROSE JOHNSON

The Reluctant Groom
Published by Sweet Rose Press
U.S.A.

Edited by Fay Lamb
Cover Design Castle Creations
Formatting by Cindy Jackson
Printed in the United States of America

Acknowledgements

I am constantly amazed by the generosity of people who are willing to help me make my books the best they can be. Special thanks goes to Edward Arrington, Beverly Lytle, and Becky Smith for proofreading this book, and Melissa Lemaire for beta reading The Reluctant Groom. You are all such a blessing to me.

I would like to thank my critique group as well for their encouragement and input. You ladies are the best!

To you the reader, thank you for your trust and time. I hope you find this story entertaining.

1

Ray O'Brien plopped a fry into his mouth and sat back against the red vinyl seat at his favorite burger joint in Seattle. An eighties song played from the jukebox in the corner. Life went on around him as though nothing was about to change, but change was approaching like a speeding train with no one manning the brakes.

He looked across the table at his buddy and confidant, Ian Parker. "I don't know what I'm going to do. My grandfather's will is ironclad." Ray wadded the pieces of the paper napkin he'd been shredding. "There's no way I'll retain ownership of the gym if I don't marry by my twenty-eighth birthday. I can't meet a woman and fall in love in so little time."

"I don't understand how someone can force another person to marry in this day and age." Ian shook his head. "There ought to be a law against it."

"No one is forcing me to get married. I only have to marry if I'm going to retain the gym. I've worked in my family's business since I was sixteen. Worked my way to the top. Nothing's been handed to me. I knew about the will's requirement but figured getting married by twenty-eight wouldn't be a problem. What a waste."

"Come on. Those weren't wasted years. You learned a lot, and you've done a ton of good helping the kids down at the community center. Not many people your age can say they own and operate two businesses and a charity foundation."

"Shh," Ray hissed as he looked around to make sure no one was paying attention. Ian's knowledge of Ray's ownership of Kids First Community Center was bad enough, but if word got out that he was personally funding it with the Kids and Youth Foundation that he secretly set up, it would change everything. People would hound him for money and treat him differently. He very much enjoyed being treated as a regular guy, and being able to support and run the center anonymously was imperative.

"Sorry. So tell me this. If you don't marry, what happens to the community center?"

That was the worst part. Too bad Gramps hadn't been able to predict the consequences of his actions. "It will cease to exist. The gym's profits support the foundation, which in turn, support the community center," he whispered.

"What about all the kids? Where will they go after school?"

He shrugged. "Their parents will have to figure it out. It's not like we're the only option."

Ian shook his head. "Maybe it's for the best."

A heavy weight sat on Ray now, but if he lost The Ring Athletic Club, and if the foundation closed, then he'd be free to start over. Starting over could be a good thing, except for one problem. He loved the people at the community center. They were like family, and they gave him purpose.

"Maybe what's for the best?" Brandi, Ian's fiancée, asked as she slid into the booth beside Ian. Her best friend, Katie Fairchild, scooted in beside him, quiet as usual.

"Ray is going to have to close his athletic club because he's not married," Ian said.

"That's nuts." Brandi scrunched her nose. "What does one have to do with the other?"

"Exactly!" Ray said. Gramps sure messed up. He explained the stipulation in his grandfather's will that whoever operated The Ring Athletic Club must be married by their twenty-eighth birthday. If his father hadn't died from a heart attack fourteen years ago leaving him or his sister next in line to run the gym, they wouldn't be having this conversation.

Katie's eyes grew round. "How can an eligible bachelor like you not have any marriage prospects?"

"Thanks, but who would marry me? I have nothing to offer. I make a modest salary, so I'm not wealthy, and I work too much."

"I'd marry you."

He whipped around to face her. "Seriously?" He liked Katie, but he could rarely get past the wall she erected around herself.

Katie's cheeks blossomed red. "I can't believe I said that. I take it back. Why not sell the business before your birthday and use the profits to open a new one?"

He couldn't take his gaze off of Katie. Her light blue eyes and pixy style hair were cute in a Tinker Bell kind of way. He didn't know much about her past, but he knew it had been difficult, and she had overcome a lot. Too bad they weren't close like their friends. Could he marry someone he didn't love in order to keep his passion solvent? But she'd recanted the offer, so it didn't matter.

He shook his head. "Using the profits would be nice, but I'd have to start from scratch. The boxing ring below the athletic club has been there for forty years. It's still used for matches and the notoriety alone that it generates in income…Let's just say it'd be hard to make that kind of profit in a new business." He ran a hand along his neck then rested his elbows on the table. "None of this would even be an issue if my sister had agreed to run The Ring. She married long before her twenty-eighth birthday." He could have worked out an arrangement with her to fund his foundation, and he wouldn't be having this conversation.

Katie nodded. "I love your sister, and her daughter is a doll. She's so tiny for a four-year–old."

He tilted his head slightly. "I didn't realize you knew them."

"We go to the same Bible study, and I watch Emily on occasion. In fact, I'm sitting for them this weekend while they're away celebrating their anniversary."

"How could I not know this?"

Ian chuckled. "Sorry, I didn't think to mention it. Your sister asked a while back if I knew anyone who might be interested in babysitting. I suggested Katie. As it turned out, they already knew each other from church."

"Small world. I've been watching Emily for them ever since," Katie said.

Her life was more woven into his than he'd realized.

Brandi pointed a finger at her friend. "You know, getting married isn't a bad idea."

"Huh?" Ray and Katie said in unison.

"Think about it. I've already sold the place where Katie and I live, and she's moving out in two weeks anyway. So far, the roommate search isn't going well. This would take care of both your problems. Is there any clause in the will that stipulates how long you must stay married?"

"Uh…I don't know."

"You need to find out."

"It doesn't matter. I'm not going to marry with the intention of divorcing after a set time."

"It wouldn't be a real marriage." Brandi rolled her eyes as if he should understand her crazy brain. "Don't you have an apartment above your garage?"

He nodded. Although it was a mess and needed a lot of TLC before anyone could live there.

"Your wife," she made air quotes, "could live in the apartment for however long you're married. You'd meet the requirement of the will, and everyone would be happy."

She might be onto something, but as a Christian, he struggled with her plan. Sure, he wanted to keep the center going, and he certainly didn't want to close The Ring, but he wouldn't marry for the sole reason of keeping his dream alive. He would find another way to fund the community center.

Brandi looked at her cell phone and gasped. "It's later than I thought. Come on, Ian. We have a dance lesson tonight."

Ian groaned. "I can't believe I let you talk me into those."

Brandi tugged on Ian's arm. "Let's go. And stop your complaining. You'll thank me on our wedding day when you're able to waltz flawlessly." She stood and looped her arm through his. "See you."

Ray slid from the booth after Katie. "You need a ride home?" He'd never seen her with a car.

Her gaze darted toward the door where Brandi had exited only seconds ago, her brow puckered. "I suppose so."

"If you'd rather walk or take the bus, that's fine. I won't be offended."

A small smile lifted her lips. "I appreciate the offer. Thanks."

"No problem." He held the door for her as they exited. "What do you think I should do?"

"What I think isn't important," she mumbled.

"It is to me."

She shot a look his way. "Why?"

"Because it is." He respected her opinion. She might not talk much, but it was clear to anyone paying attention she was wise beyond her years.

"Listen to your heart. What I think doesn't matter."

He had no idea what his heart was telling him other than he couldn't marry for the sake of his charity. "Your opinion matters to me."

She looked at him with surprise in her eyes. "You should do what you think is best. After all, it's your life, not mine."

"That's not helpful." He pulled the key toggle from his pocket and unlocked the doors to his five-year-old black Honda.

Katie slid into the front seat before he could open the door for her. She was young, twenty-three, if memory served, and had never finished college. He'd once asked her why she'd quit, but she avoided answering the question as well as a politician. He slid behind the wheel and buckled up. "Last I heard you were working at a coffee shop. Are you still there?"

"No. I took a job at the community center down the block from The Ring. I'm hoping it will turn into a fulltime position. I love it there."

His gaze shot her way.

"What? Did I say something wrong?"

His pulse jumped. "No. You surprised me. That's all." He turned his head forward. How could he not know that he employed Katie? His manager had mentioned hiring a new girl, Kaitlyn something. Of course, Katie was short for Kaitlyn, but he'd never made the connection. He cleared his throat. "What do you do there?" There were only three paid staffers—the director and then two part-time workers. He didn't need to ask the question since he knew what position was filled, but he was still curious about her answer.

"I'm in charge of the elementary age kids' programs."

"Do you like it?"

"I love it! I only wish it was full time. I never should have quit my job at the coffee shop. It definitely wasn't one of my smarter decisions, but I hated it there."

"I'm sorry. Are you trying to find other work?"

"Yes. I even had an interview, but the hours conflicted with my current job, and I didn't want to give it up."

"I see. We might have an opening at The Ring. Have you applied there?"

"I didn't think of it. Thanks for the tip. But if you don't get married, isn't it going to close?"

"From what I understand, yes, but I'm not sure. I need to meet with the attorney to know with absolute certainty." He also wanted to thoroughly read the will for himself once he procured a copy. One thing was certain; he couldn't let down all the people who depended on him. Somehow he had to save The Ring and the community center. He'd been to Brandi and Katie's condo a few times, so he knew how to get there, but he deliberately took the long way—Katie's sweet, soft voice soothed him. "What kind of things do you do with the kids at the community center?"

"I plan outings and activities. Do welfare checks—"

Whoa. "What do you mean welfare checks?" None of the employees were supposed to have contact with the kids outside the center.

She shrugged. "It's nothing. Once in a while I get concerned about a kid, so I drop a meal or a bag of groceries by their home."

"Do the families know you do it?"

"Sometimes. Other times, I leave the bag and run."

"But how? You don't have a car?"

She grinned. "Brandi helps me. It's actually fun. But I guess I won't be able to do that once she moves to England." Her voice faded off as if she realized for the first time she wouldn't have her co-conspirator for much longer.

"It's too bad about Brandi, but I'm curious—how do you know who needs food?"

"I listen more than I talk when I'm at work," she said simply, as if it were nothing. He could testify to the truth of her words. She was a quiet person, but when she did speak, she made her words count.

He pulled up to her complex. "I'll walk you to your place."

"No need." She hopped out and shut the door.

Before he could even turn off the engine, she'd darted out of sight. He shook his head and drove toward home. She was technically breaking the rules by delivering food to the kids, but he couldn't fault her. She had a big heart—much like him. He couldn't shake her earlier offer. Would she be willing to partner with him permanently for the sake of the children?

Katie leaned against her condo door. Her heart raced. Why did Ray have such an effect on her? She thought she was over him. This schoolgirl crush she had on him must stop. She couldn't believe she'd been able to carry on a conversation with him after telling him she'd marry him. She bumped the back of her head against the door several times. He probably thought she was pathetic, throwing herself at him like that.

In spite of his claim that no woman would want to marry him, she was sure he must have women calling him all the time. In fact, he was dating someone not all that long ago. Then again she hadn't seen or heard mention of the woman for at least six months.

Ray was a cool guy who didn't know he was cool. Even though he was the owner of a fitness club, he wasn't a complete fitness nut who obsessed over his body constantly. Although he took care of himself, which she and probably every other single woman he knew appreciated, to her way of thinking, his clean-cut, dark hair, and brown eyes were his best features.

"Stop." She could not keep dreaming about him. He was a nice guy and Ian's best friend. They would walk down the aisle as best man and maid of honor together—and that was it. There'd be no wedding bells in their future.

Starving since the diner they were at didn't cater to the gluten-free crowd, she grabbed a gluten-free meal from the freezer and popped it into the microwave. She loved these entrées and since they were organic it eased the guilt of eating a frozen meal rather than making something fresh.

Five minutes later, she moseyed into her tiny bedroom holding a plate containing her dinner. After flipping on the radio, she took a quick bite of the Mexican casserole as she sat at the built-in desk where her computer was. *Mmm.* She never tired of this dish. She went to her e-mail to check for prospective roommate applicants and devoured her meal while clicking on the single response—a male. She sighed and pressed delete. Couldn't people read? She specifically stated the opening was for a female.

When Brandi said she was moving to England and selling her condo, Katie never imagined how difficult moving and finding another roommate would be. Maybe she was going about this wrong. Perhaps she should be responding to roommate-needed ads since her low income had been preventing her applications from being accepted.

Then again, if she could land a second job, a roommate might not be an issue. She navigated over to a jobs listing and scrolled down the screen. Nothing looked interesting, but at this point, she couldn't afford to be picky.

An hour later, the door to the condo opened and clicked shut. "Brandi?"

"Yes. It's me." A moment later, her friend stood in her doorway holding a pair of dance shoes.

"How was the lesson?"

"Okay. Don't tell Ian I said this, but he's a better dancer than me."

"Then why the lessons?"

A tiny smile touched her lips. "I love being in his arms." A dreamy look covered her face then cleared. "Plus it's good practice." She came into the room and looked over Katie's shoulder at the computer screen. "You find anything?"

"I applied to be a maid at a hotel downtown."

Brandi wrinkled her nose. "You'd hate that job."

"That's beside the point. Ray mentioned a position at The Ring. I couldn't find it listed online, so I'll drop in there tomorrow. If the hours are right, it could be exactly what I've been looking for." Even if it ended up being temporary, it could buy her some time.

Brandi sat on the edge of Katie's twin bed. "You and Ray visited after we left?"

"He gave me a ride."

She bit her lip. "I was supposed to do that. I'm sorry I forgot."

"It's fine. He offered."

"Ray's a good guy. I hope he can figure something out so he can keep his business open."

"Me, too, especially if I get a job there and it closes. I'll be back in the same situation I am now."

"True. Maybe working at The Ring isn't a good idea."

But it might be fun—depending on what she'd be doing. "It's a job, and that's all I care about right now."

Thankfully, she'd never shared her crush on Ray with her friend, although sometimes she wondered if Brandi knew but never said anything.

Brandi yawned and stood. "I have an early morning. Good night."

"'Night." She shut down the computer and jumped when her phone chimed. She checked the screen.

CAN YOU MEET ME AT THE RING TOMORROW AT ONE? RAY.

Why would Ray want to meet with her? Maybe he had a job offer!

"Sure. See you then."

2

Ray hung up his desk phone at the athletic club after talking with his grandfather's attorney and scheduling an appointment for later in the morning. His birthday was three months away, and decisions had to be made soon.

He glanced at the clock on the wall in his office and stood. He'd head out now and check in at the community center on the way. He closed and locked his office door then headed downstairs to the main level.

"Ray, do you have a minute?" Tasha, the front desk attendant, strode toward him.

"Just. What's up?"

"Did you look over the proposal I gave you?"

He rubbed the back of his neck. Here and now was not the time to have this conversation. "I did. Can we talk when I get back?" He and everyone else at the gym thought highly of Tasha, but she was overqualified for the position, and it looked as if she was determined to put her degree to use at The Ring. Well, he didn't need her expertise—he needed a miracle.

The hopeful look on her face fell. "You didn't like it."

"That's not it." He looked around to see who might be listening, but no one loitered nearby. "Your proposal was solid, but this isn't a good time for me to consider expanding. I'm sorry."

Tasha's head dipped. "Okay. But if anything changes—"

"I'll let you know. I have an appointment, but I'll be back by one." He left without waiting for a reply. He hated to disappoint her. He knew she wanted to run her own gym. She'd do a great job, too, but opening a second gym didn't fit his business plan. He could never replicate what they had at The Ring.

He strode along the sidewalk. A garbage truck rumbled past leaving an unsavory smell in its wake. A seagull landed on a garbage can chained to a tree. At the end of the block his trek ended. He unlocked the front door of the center and pushed inside. The door closed, blocking out the city noise. He breathed in deeply, taking in the smell of pine-scented cleaner and a hint of sweat as he walked down a short hallway. The basketball court was to his left where people of all ages played nearly every evening year round, and the activity rooms were to his right with large windows facing the hall so people could see both in and out. The rooms were used for arts and crafts, movies, birthday parties, special guests such as musicians, and once a children's author came to read to the kids.

He grinned, thinking about the quality activities the center offered as he walked further into the building. The quiet of the morning before the place got busy was always his favorite time since it gave him the opportunity to look things over before the manager arrived. The circle of people who knew he owned the center was small and only included his attorney, the manager of the community center who had signed a confidentiality agreement, and Ian.

At the manager's desk, Ray clicked on the computer. He still couldn't believe he didn't know Katie worked here. Then again, with direct deposit and the fact he'd hired a bookkeeper, there was no way he'd know unless they'd been here at the same time, which clearly hadn't happened.

He found the file he was looking for, clicked it open, and skimmed through the information. Katie Fairchild. Age twenty-three, high school graduate, completed one year of college. Her resume listed odd jobs but nothing impressive. She'd been working at the center for the past eight weeks. Her hobbies included, art, theater, music, baking, and running marathons. *Hmm.*

He signed off the computer, scribbled out a note to his manager, Gary, letting him know he'd been by and used the computer. Then he made sure everything looked in order. Satisfied the place met his expectations, he left via the back door, which led to an alley he and the other property owners worked hard to maintain. Colorful graffiti covered the wall of the building behind his, but unlike many areas in Seattle, this alley wasn't sketchy. He walked the short distance to The Ring and got into his Honda.

The typical Friday morning traffic slowed him, but he made it to his ten o'clock appointment right on time. He walked into the attorney's office. "Good morning, Aaron."

"Have a seat, Ray. I'll get straight to the point." He handed him an envelope. "Upon the announcement of your engagement you were to have received this letter from your grandfather, but it seems that isn't going to happen, so I'm giving it to you now. Once you're finished reading it, I'll answer your questions to the best of my ability."

Ray's shoulders tightened as he slipped his finger under the flap and tore down the side of the envelope. He pulled out a single sheet of handwritten paper.

Grandson,

I can't tell you how proud I am of you. Marriage is not something to be taken lightly, but I'm sure you have given this a lot of thought, and I know the woman you chose will be the helpmate in business and in life that you need.

There is something to be said for the love of a good woman. You may have wondered why I insisted you marry by your twenty-eighth birthday in order to retain ownership of The Ring, and the answer is simple.

Life is too short to spend it alone in that office working day and night. I learned that the hard way, and your grandmother was the one to teach me. I want you to live a happy and fulfilled life with a family, not stuck at work all the time.

To be honest, I feared you would never see this letter, and that you would choose instead to remain single. You are a driven man, and I thought you might choose to sell the business and start over.

He looked up and focused on his grandfather's attorney. "What does he mean, sell and start over? That's an option? Could I sell The Ring and reinvest the money into something different?" That would solve his problem.

"No."

"Then why show me this?"

"I thought if, by chance, there was any woman in your life that you might be swayed to act sooner than later. He stipulated in his will that should you not marry, the business would be sold and the profits would be donated to cancer research."

Ray let out the breath he'd been holding. His grandmother had died of cancer. It made sense that Gramps would stipulate the money went there. "So either I marry or I lose everything. That's what he meant by starting over?"

Aaron nodded. "His hope was that it wouldn't come to that. I'm sorry. I know this puts you in a difficult situation, but if it's any consolation, he did stipulate that you would receive ten percent of the profits. That should be enough to give you a bit of seed money or tide you over long enough to find work."

He nodded and kept reading.

I'm glad you didn't. The Ring is a special place. The history there is also pretty special, as you know.

Well, that's it, Grandson. Well done and congratulations.

He let it drop into his lap.

"Would you like me to take care of the sale for you?" Aaron steepled his fingers and raised a brow.

Ray blinked and focused on his grandfather's long-time attorney. "Don't do anything."

"The will is ironclad. Either you marry or it must be sold. Unless you have a bride that I don't know about, it's time to start letting your customers and employees know that The Ring will be closing."

"I'd like a copy of the will."

"I suspected you might." He opened a file and pulled out a multi-page document. "It won't change anything."

We'll see. There had to be some way to keep the community center open. "Thank you." He stood and offered his hand. "I'll be in touch."

"You're only prolonging the inevitable." Aaron's mouth pulled down into a frown.

"Perhaps." He left the attorney and went straight for his car. If he returned to the club, he'd get non-stop interruptions from Tasha. Instead, he headed to his favorite deli for an early lunch and quiet reading time. He might not be an attorney, but he'd taken several business classes in college that enabled him to understand legalese.

A short time later, he took a window seat that faced the Sound and read the contract word for word. The more he read, the more his chest ached. He understood why his grandfather had done this—Gramps didn't know that since Ray had taken over The Ring Athletic Club he'd funneled a generous portion of the profits into a charity foundation. Sure he'd known a large chunk of money went to charity, but not where.

Ray took a deep breath and let it out slowly. He'd prayed after leaving Katie last night and felt the Lord nudge him to meet with her today, but for the life of him he had no idea what he was going to say. Could he really do what he was thinking?

Lord, if I heard you wrong, please stop me from making a huge mistake. He stood, tossed his garbage, and headed back to The Ring to meet with Katie.

Katie took extra care with her appearance today. She applied a pale color of lipstick, pressed her lips together, and then she ran the mascara brush over her lashes. She didn't wear much makeup but always wore lipstick and mascara. She had no idea why Ray wanted to meet her, but one thing was certain, it was important. He'd never sought out her company before. More than likely, he wanted to discuss best man and maid of honor business. But why hadn't he mentioned it last night? Although she didn't mind brainstorming their friends' wedding stuff with him, she hoped he wanted to talk about a job.

She slipped on her favorite consignment shop find—a like-new Burberry London trench coat she had picked up for a steal. Her last foster mom told her if she wore a nice coat it didn't matter what she had on under it. Good advice or not, she'd purchased the coat with all the high school graduation money she'd received and had treasured it since.

She grabbed her purse and rushed out the door. The bus would be at the corner in five minutes, and she couldn't afford to miss it. The clouds overhead threatened rain but so far nothing. She spotted the bus in the distance and quickened her pace. Her boots clicked on the concrete. The bus whooshed to a stop. She stepped on, scanned her pass, then found a seat near the front.

Taking the bus kind of stunk, but it was the most practical way to get around the city. Besides, it wasn't like she had money to waste on a car and insurance.

Her stomach fluttered with nerves. In under an hour, she'd find out what was up with Ray, and she had a feeling it was big, even if it concerned their friends' wedding.

Finally, the bus came to her stop. She got off and walked the half-block to The Ring—such an odd name for an athletic club. She'd have to ask him about that choice.

She'd admired Ray since she'd met him two years ago. Okay, she more than admired him, but it didn't matter. A man like him would never be interested in a girl like her with nothing to show for her life, who had deadbeat parents who probably didn't even remember they had a daughter. Not that she cared—she was better off without them.

She pushed the club's glass door open. "Whoa." How had she never come in here before? This place was huge—much bigger on the inside than it looked from the sidewalk. She meandered to the reception desk situated about twenty feet from the entrance.

A woman with long, brunette hair, who looked to be only a few years older than Katie, smiled at her. "Good afternoon. May I help you?"

"I have a meeting with Ray at one."

"I'll let him know you're here. Feel free to look around while you wait." She pulled out her cell and shot off a text.

Katie wandered into the weight room and noted both free weights and machines. She stepped out of the room and heard her name.

"Sorry I'm late." Ray rushed over to her slightly winded. "Traffic was slower than I expected. Let's talk in my office." He led the way upstairs and unlocked a door.

She wasn't sure what she'd expected, but this wasn't it. A metal desk sat in the center facing the door. A large window looked out into the club from above, and two chairs that appeared to be from the fifties faced the desk. She walked to the window and swayed as sudden dizziness hit her.

Two hands grasped her upper arms from behind. "Easy there. Are you afraid of heights?"

She turned away from the window to face Ray. "I didn't think so."

"How about we sit and talk over here away from the window?"

"Good idea." What had come over her? She was healthy and strong, never fainted, and never got vertigo. So weird. She sat in one of the chairs intended for visitors, and he took the other one.

"I went to see my grandfather's attorney this morning."

"Any good news?"

"That depends."

"On?" Why did he look like he'd rather be running a marathon in the heat of summer than sitting here talking with her?

"You."

"Me? I thought you asked me here to talk about the wedding."

"Wedding!" A woman stood in the doorway. Her face couldn't look more shocked. "No wonder you don't want to expand the business right now."

Ray's brow furrowed. "Did you need something, Tasha?"

"Ah. No. It'll keep until you're done talking with your fiancée."

"Please close the door on your way out."

"That was awkward. Why didn't you correct her?"

He rubbed the back of his neck. "I'd rather she think I'm engaged."

"I see. But I don't understand why I'm here if not to discuss the wedding."

"I've changed my mind." He stood. "I'm sorry for asking you to meet me. I…" He opened and closed his mouth. Then he ushered her to the door. "Will you see yourself out?"

"Of course." What had happened? And what about that job he mentioned?

3

Later that same week, Katie walked into her friends' house with her suitcase in hand. Emily ran toward her. Katie set her luggage down and opened her arms. "Hello precious." She stood holding the feather light little girl in her arms. "Are you ready to have a fun weekend?"

"Yes. Mommy said we can go to the donut shop." Her brown eyes grew large. "I love chocolate with sprinkles."

Renee, her mother, chuckled. "That's the truth. How about you go and play in your bedroom while Mommy talks with Katie."

Katie set the child on the floor. "I'll come find you in a bit." This weekend was going to be fun. Plus, she was getting paid, which was a bonus as far as she was concerned.

"We can't thank you enough for watching Emily. We're only going to play tourists here in Seattle, but I'm so excited. Our hotel is this little boutique place downtown. We haven't been able to get away for a whole weekend since before she was born."

"You're kidding! What about your family?"

Renee waved a hand. "I would never ask my mom. She has no clue what to do with a child. I should know. My sister, Hailey, is only nineteen and lives with my mom, and my brother would be lost. Ray is wonderful for a few hours but an entire weekend?" She shuddered. "He'd run out of things to do with her and beg me to come home early."

Katie frowned. "I imagine he'd figure it out."

Renee sobered. "You're right. He would. Come into the kitchen. I made a list and want to go through it with you."

"You and your lists." Ever since she first met Renee, the woman had a list of some sort with her at all times.

"You'll thank me later when you don't know which cup is Emily's favorite or where to find her favorite video or—"

"I get it. Walk me through everything." For the next thirty minutes she listened as Renee went point by point through a two-page list. What had she gotten herself into? She had no idea taking care of one little girl could be so much work. When she'd watched Emily in the past, it had only been for an hour or two and the list of instructions had been much smaller.

"Questions?"

"When will you be back?" Katie asked.

"Sunday afternoon." Renee rested a hand on Katie's arm. "I know I already said it, but thank you. This means so much to us."

"You're welcome. After all, what are friends for if not to provide childcare for a romantic getaway?"

"Speaking of which. When are you going to let me set you up on a blind date with my brother? He's a few years older than you, but I think the two of you would hit it off."

Time to come clean. She'd known for a while that her friend was Ray's sister but had never revealed that bit of information. "Actually, Ray and I have known one another for a while. He's good friends with my best friend's fiancé."

Renee squealed. "What? And you never said anything?"

"Hon." Matt, Renee's husband walked into the kitchen. "We need to get moving. Traffic is terrible." He sidled up to his wife and drew her close with an arm wrapped around her waist.

Renee rested her head against his shoulder for a moment then pulled away. "Okay. If you think of any questions, you have our cell numbers."

"Right. Don't worry. Emily and I are going to have a great weekend. I thought we might even take the bus to the zoo."

"Sounds like fun," Matt said. "Now let's go." He tugged on his wife's hand. "See you Sunday, Katie." They said good-bye to their daughter, who took their leaving surprisingly well.

Katie found Emily playing dolls in her bedroom. She couldn't remember being four but imagined she played much the same as this little one. Had her mom played with her? If only she could remember back that far. But those early years were fuzzy. Mom definitely didn't play later on. In fact, she didn't like it when Katie played with dolls.

Katie would let Emily play until she got bored then she'd pull out her bag with coloring books and crayons. She'd rented a couple of movies just in case. Although accustomed to kids, the youngest children at the community center were a couple of years older than Emily, so she was a little out of her element as far as entertaining for a long period of time. At least Ray could be called on if she got desperate—point number ten on Renee's list. Katie chuckled and wondered if Ray was as obsessive about lists as his older sister.

Somehow, she doubted it. Sure, he was stressed about the athletic club right now, and whether he should get married or not, but generally he was confident and grounded. What had possessed her to offer to marry him? If he'd pursued the issue, would she have agreed? It wasn't like there was a line of men waiting to take her out. Why was that? What was wrong with her that men never waded past the shield of distrust that shrouded her? There had to be someone out there who cared enough to venture past the surface.

"I'm bored," Emily said as she crawled up beside her on the couch in the family room.

"Hmm." Katie glanced at the clock on the wall. "It's seven-thirty and time to get ready for bed. How about you take a bath and brush your teeth? Then I'll read you a story." Renee had warned her that Emily fought her when it came to baths. She held her breath, hoping it wouldn't be an issue tonight.

"Two stories?" Emily grinned.

"Okay. Two, but you need to move fast. Your mom said you needed to be in bed at eight."

"Okie-dokie." She raced into the bathroom.

Katie followed, pleased at how easy that had been. Twenty minutes later, Emily was tucked in bed, bright-eyed and awaiting the stories. She picked up the first book Emily had requested, *Sammy the Seal*. She read the story and before long, Emily's eyelids drooped.

She yawned. "I love you, Katie."

"I love you, too, little one. Are you sure you want two stories tonight?"

She nodded and rolled over, closing her eyes.

Katie made it to the second page before Emily was out. Oh to be able to fall asleep that easily.

"Sweet dreams." She placed a kiss on the child's head before switching on the nightlight and leaving the room. Emily was one of the sweetest children she'd ever known. Matt and Renee had done a great job raising her. Maybe she'd get the chance to raise a child of her own one-day. But first things first—she needed a man.

Ray took a moment to compose himself and wipe the tears from his eyes as he stood outside his brother-in-law's ICU hospital room. He'd come as soon as he'd gotten the call that there'd been an accident. But he only learned moments ago that his sister had been killed instantly. A sob tore though him. He had to get it together. Matt needed him. He took a deep, shuddering breath and let it out slowly. *Lord, I need Your help. I'm not strong enough on my own.*

He pushed into the room and caught his breath at the sight of Matt connected to various machines he couldn't name. His black eye was swollen shut and the other looked almost there, too. He cleared his throat. "Hey, buddy."

"You came." His voice was weak.

"Of course. I wish I would've known sooner. I'd have been here hours ago."

"I was in surgery." A tear slid down his face. He didn't bother to brush it away. "Renee, she—"

"I know." He blinked back tears. His heart hurt as he sat beside Matt's hospital bed. This was not supposed to happen. He'd spoken with his sister only yesterday, and now she was dead. In a split second, his sister's life had been snuffed out thanks to a drunk driver, and his brother-in-law's prognosis was not good.

Matt looked at him with pleading eyes. "Please take good care of Emily. She loves you nearly as much as us. You're all she has left."

Matt never talked about his family. He'd assumed his brother-in-law had parents, but they hadn't been at his wedding, so maybe he'd assumed wrong. "There's my mom and Hailey, plus you're still here. Fight to live, Matt. Your daughter needs you. But I'll always be there for both of you. I love that munchkin, and you're not so bad yourself," he teased, trying to lighten the mood even though all he wanted to do was weep.

"Everything's in the will." Matt labored to breath. "Don't let the state put her in foster care. You're her guardian." His final word came out in a whisper. Then alarms went off all around him.

A nurse rushed him. "Sir, you need to step into the hall."

Ray's stomach knotted. He moved aside as several other medical staff poured into the room. He stood by, helpless. His throat thickened, and his eyes burned. This could not be real. It had to be a bad dream—no—a nightmare. He slipped from the room as a doctor barked orders. Matt couldn't die, too. Emily needed him. They both needed him. He couldn't raise his sweet niece on his own. His family would be little help. He'd already lost so much. His future was unsure. How much grief could one person bear? Matt had to live.

A short time later the doctor walked out and shook his head. "I'm sorry."

His throat too thick to speak, Ray only nodded and turned away, brushing a hand across his eyes. His hands fisted. It wasn't fair. In a span of ten hours, he'd lost his sister and his brother-in-law, and his four-year-old niece had become an orphan.

"Ray!" Katie rushed to his side. "I came as fast as I could. How are they? I left Emily with a nurse, so we could talk privately."

He blinked back tears, cleared his throat, and shook his head. "They didn't make it."

She caught her breath. "Oh no. I'm so sorry." She placed a hand on his arm. Tears welled in her eyes, and she shot a glance toward the nurse's station.

He followed her gaze, which rested on his four-year-old niece as she visited with one of the nurses. "We need to be strong for Emily."

Katie nodded. "Of course." She took a breath and let it out in a puff. "Give me a minute," her voice broke. "I need to collect myself before facing Emily." She walked to the end of the hall.

He stood there torn between comforting Katie and going to his niece. Emily had to come first, but he needed Katie's moral support. He waited until she returned. Her red-rimmed eyes were now dry, but it was obvious she'd been crying.

"Are you ready?" He nodded toward his niece.

"No, but there's no use prolonging the inevitable. I think we should tell her back at her house though, not here."

"That's probably a good idea. Why does she think you're here?"

"I told her I needed to go visit a friend."

He nodded. "How'd you get here?"

"The bus."

"You and Emily will ride with me. Let's go."

Ray focused on the road as he drove to his sister's house. Emily sat in the backseat singing, completely oblivious to how her world was about to change. Katie sat somberly beside him.

He needed to tell his mom and younger sister, too.

He was listed as the emergency contact that his sister had on record at the hospital from when she'd given birth to Emily, so he'd been the one notified. How was he supposed to tell everyone about Renee and Matt? Ease into it, or blurt it out like ripping off a bandage? He glanced toward Katie and noticed her eyes were closed. He reached over and took her hand. "You okay?"

She startled and opened her eyes. "No. You?"

"I've been better. I don't know how to do this."

"You mean uh…deliver bad news?" Clearly, she was choosing her words carefully.

"Yes."

"I don't know either. I guess explain what happened. Do you want me there?"

Good question. Although his niece clearly adored her, would asking Katie to stay be fair? Probably not. "Thanks, but I think it's something I need to do alone."

"I understand. If you need anything just ask."

"I can give you a ride home."

"Not necessary. I'll grab my stuff and take the bus. That's how I got there."

"Is Katie going home?" Emily's brow puckered and her bottom lip protruded as he looked in his rearview mirror. "What about the zoo?"

Katie shifted to face Emily better. "There's been a change in plans, sweetie. Your uncle Ray is going to be with you today instead, and I'm going to go home."

"But I want you, too."

"Maybe you should stick around after all. The two of you seem to have a connection. That might be helpful later." He shot a quick glance her way and noticed indecision written on her face. "That is, if you don't mind."

"It's fine. I can stay."

"Yay! Can we go to the zoo now?"

"No, we can't. We're going to Grandma's." He tried to sound excited about the prospect, but on a good day, he didn't enjoy visiting his mom. Now that Katie was sticking around, there was no reason to put off the inevitable any longer.

"Oh," Emily said.

Katie frowned. "You don't want to see your grandma?"

"I want to go to the zoo. Maybe Grandma will want to go." She looked pleased at the idea.

He stayed quiet and changed course. They'd be at his mom and sister's place in a matter of minutes. It was still early for a Saturday. Hopefully, they'd be up and dressed. Otherwise, Mom would never forgive him for bringing a stranger into her home unannounced, not even under these circumstances.

4

A week after Matt and Renee's joint funeral, Katie stood outside The Ring and took a deep breath then let it out. *You are strong and brave. You can do this!* She pulled open the door and marched inside. The same woman who'd interrupted her and Ray the last time she was there stood at the counter.

"Good morning. May I help you?"

"Yes. I'm here to see Ray. Is he available?" She hadn't seen him since the funeral, although she'd called to check on Emily a couple of times. Her heart hurt for the little girl and her uncle, but it was time to move forward. She missed Renee, but if years in foster care taught her one thing, it was that people came and went and to not get too attached. Although she was in serious risk of getting too attached right now.

"He's in his office. You're welcome to go up and surprise him."

"Okay. Thanks." She wasn't sure that was a good idea but went along with the suggestion. She rapped on the closed door.

"Come in."

The sound of Ray's deep bass sent butterfly wings fluttering in her stomach. She pushed open the door and walked in, head held high.

His eyes widened, and he bolted to his feet. "Katie! I wasn't expecting you."

"Surprise. May I sit?" She motioned to the same chair she'd occupied the last time.

"Of course. How are you?" He stepped around his desk, closed the door, then sat in the chair beside her.

"I'm fine." She had to get this out before she lost her nerve. "Here's the thing. You need help with Emily and you need a wife. If you'll have me, I'll marry you." The words rushed from her lips so fast she wasn't sure he'd understood. Plus, the blank look on his face made her wonder. She forced herself to speak slowly and clearly. "I said I'll marry you."

He shook his head as if he was coming out of a daze. "I heard you the first time. I'm in shock."

"I know a lot has happened since that night at the diner, and if you've changed your mind about needing a wife, I'll understand." Her face burned. She never should have come here. "I'm not trying to throw myself at you. It's Emily. She needs—"

"You."

Her gaze shot to his. His soulful eyes told her everything she needed to know for now. He needed her, too. They needed each other.

"Are you sure? Because if you're not, walk away

right now. Emily and I have had more than enough heartbreak, and I don't think either of us could handle more."

How could she break his heart? He'd have to love her for that to happen. Could he be insinuating that? Impossible. He'd never indicated he felt anything more than casual friendship.

She nodded. "I have one request. If we're going to do this, we need to get to know each other better. I feel like I know you, but you don't know me at all. Well, at least not that well." She snapped her mouth shut at the intense look in his eyes. Had she said too much?

He nodded. "I suppose you're right. But I need help with Emily now. I took the last two weeks off, but she's with my mom today. Renee and my mom didn't see life through the same lens, and she wouldn't be happy to know Mom is the only childcare I could arrange."

"So you want me to be what…your live-in nanny?" She'd offered to be his wife. Not exactly a hardship to her way of thinking, but still—she was giving up a lot. Including her pride.

His face lit. "That's exactly what I need."

"But what about your grandfather's will and the business?"

He frowned. "Good point. My birthday is exactly seventy days away."

Katie straightened. "You're counting?" She had a birthday coming up, but she didn't like to think of those since her past birthdays had been less than memorable.

"Wouldn't you be if you were in my position?"

He had a point. She might even be counting down the hours.

"What if you move into the apartment above my garage?"

"I don't understand. How does this help your situation?"

He stood and walked around to the other side of his desk and took the seat beside her. "This is the perfect arrangement. You wanted me to get to know you before we marry, and I need a nanny, housekeeper, and cook, and someone to share this with, if you're up for all of that. I would pay you, of course, and your room and board would be free. While we're getting to know one another, we'll plan our wedding and get married a week or two before my birthday. I'll have met the requirements of the will, and we'll have had the opportunity to figure out if we're making the biggest mistake of our lives or if moving forward with the wedding is the right thing to do."

So he did want to marry her. Good. For a minute she thought he'd only wanted a nanny. "I cook gluten free." So many people thought gluten-free food was horrible, but she had no choice and didn't care to become a short-order cook.

"I remember that about you. It's fine. I'll eat what you eat and probably be healthier."

"Good. Thanks. I like your idea about me living over the garage, but Brandi won't be here when we get married. A girl's best friend should be at her wedding. She'll already be in England."

"Ian won't be here either. We don't need our best friends to get married."

"True." But she wanted Brandi to be there. Her friend was her rock. The only person she'd been able to count on no matter what. All that was about to change once her friend married Ian and he whisked her off the continent. She had to get used to doing things without Brandi. "Okay. You make a solid argument. I accept your terms." Rushing into marriage simply so her best friend could be there was foolhardy. They needed to take time to get to know one another on a more personal level.

Ray grinned. "Thank you. Now let's agree that if one of us has reservations about getting married we'll tell the other. I absolutely want to keep the athletic club in the family, but it's not worth ruining either of our lives over."

She thrust out her hand. "Agreed."

He shook it. "When can you move in?"

"Tonight, I guess. What about my job at the community center? I don't want to quit."

"Hmm." He rubbed the stubble on his chin. "Why not bring Emily with you? She'd love it."

How could she do her job and watch a four-year-old? "There's a ballet and tap class that meets there three days a week while I'm working. We should enroll Emily. She'd love it, and it would give her something fun to do while I'm working."

"Good thinking. I'll take care of that today." He leaned forward, grabbed a pen, and scribbled onto a piece of scratch paper. "Do you realize this is the most we've talked in one sitting? In fact, this is the best conversation we've ever had."

She raised a brow with a half-smile. "I take a while to warm up to people. But once I do, watch out. I've been told I talk too much."

A lopsided grin covered his face. "Impossible."

"What?" Her heart felt like a herd of racing mustangs.

"There is no way you could ever talk too much. You don't talk simply to hear yourself. When you speak, you have something to say." He shrugged. "So it's impossible that you'd ever talk too much to me."

Getting to know Ray would be interesting. More than likely, he'd change his mind about her being quiet after a week. Brandi said she had a motor mouth sometimes. She stood. "I'll let you get back to work."

Ray's pulse thrummed in his ears. Katie stood and walked toward his office door. A tingle zipped through him. He was getting married! She'd surprised him, and now everything was going to be okay. Well, almost okay. Life would never be the same after losing his sister and brother-in-law, but they were at least on the track to a new normal.

He stood and strode to her side, reaching for her hand. "Don't leave, Katie. Let's go ring shopping. We need to announce our engagement, and people will expect to see a ring on your finger."

"Oh. I didn't think of that." Her sweet and innocent blue eyes met his gaze. She blinked long lashes. "Are you sure?"

He caught his breath. He'd always thought she was cute, but up close like this, she was truly beautiful. How had he not noticed before? He cleared his throat. "Yes. If you're free, we could go now."

"Really?" Her voice hitched. "Okay. But I don't get paid until next Friday, so I can't buy your ring right now."

"Men don't wear engagement rings, so don't sweat it."

"Cute, but I was talking about getting your wedding ring."

"Okay." He knew how much she made, and there was no way he was going to let her pay for his wedding ring. Not after everything she was giving up for him and Emily. "How about you let me pay for my wedding band if we come across one? After all, you're doing this for me."

She narrowed her eyes. "No. I want to pay for your ring. But I'll need a loan until payday."

He let out the breath he'd been holding. "If you insist on paying, I'll deduct it from your wages for being Emily's nanny." He'd adjust her wages to cover the ring, and she'd be none the wiser. He'd never realized how stubborn she was.

"That works. Thank you."

He motioned for her to precede him. "After you." He followed her down the stairs, told Tasha he'd be back after lunch, and they left. He needed to get to know his future wife because he clearly didn't know her as well as he'd thought. He never imagined she'd fight him on paying for his ring.

Based on what he could dig up on her, she grew up in foster care and had little money and no family listed in her emergency contact information—although how she afforded that couture jacket she always wore, he had no idea. Tasha commented about her coat the last time she'd been in. Otherwise he'd have had no idea. He hadn't been able to glean much of anything else about Katie, though he'd only perused her employee file and spoken briefly with Ian last night. But Ian said that Brandi had been taking care of Katie since they graduated high school. What did he mean by *taking care of*?

Though seeing the petite woman at his side now, he wondered how accurate Ian's assessment had been. It could be Ian was being overly protective of his future wife. They walked a few blocks until they came to a pawnshop, and Katie dragged him inside. This wasn't the kind of place he planned to buy her ring. What were they doing here?

Katie seemed to know her way around the store and went directly to a window display of rings.

A burly dude approached them. "Hey there, Kaitlyn. What brings you by today? You have something to sell?"

"Not today, Tom. We're ring shopping. I'm looking to buy a man's wedding band."

Tom's gaze shot to Ray. "For you?"

Ray nodded and placed a hand across Katie's back. He didn't like the look of this guy. And what was with him calling her Kaitlyn? Sure, it was her legal name, but no one called her that.

Katie looked up at him. Uncertainty covered her face. "Do you mind a used ring?"

"Not used," Tom corrected. "Vintage." The dude grinned like he'd said something genius.

"A vintage ring is fine."

She beamed a breath-stealing smile at him. "Good. In that case, we'd like to see that one, Tom." She pointed to a classic man's wedding band that looked to be platinum.

"Excellent choice." Tom handed him the ring. "How about you, mister. We have some nice ladies rings."

"Uh. No, thank you." He much preferred to buy Katie's from a jewelry store. Ray slid it on his ring finger. "It's a perfect fit." He held out his hand and studied the ring.

"I knew it!" Katie beamed. "We'll take it."

"Don't you want to know the price first? This is platinum, and it's four-hundred dollars."

"Will you take three hundred?"

He shook his head. "Not even for you."

Katie frowned. "Okay. Let's go, Ray."

"Wait. That's it? No counter offer?" Tom asked.

She shook her head. "I can only do three."

He rubbed his bearded chin. "I shouldn't do this, but you're a good customer. You bought yourself a ring."

She grinned wide. "Thanks." Then she shot a panicked look at Ray and motioned him close. She whispered in his ear. "I don't have three-hundred dollars, and I don't want him to see you pay for it."

Ray stood to his full height of five-feet-ten inches. "Katie needs to go to the ATM. Will you hold onto that for a few minutes?"

"No problem. I'll get the paperwork ready."

"Thanks." He grasped her hand and gently pulled her toward the door.

"You're a lifesaver. Thanks for not embarrassing me in there. You don't happen to have three hundred on you?"

"Nope." He drew her toward the crosswalk. "My bank is around the corner." Ten minutes later they were back at the pawnshop.

Katie paid Tom and tucked the ring into her purse. "Thanks, Tom." She waved as they left the store.

"What's the story with that guy? I got the impression you're a regular."

She nodded. "I am. Aside from picking up little things from time to time, I go to garage sales on the weekends, find bargains, fix them up, then pawn them at Tom's shop."

He couldn't help being impressed. "That's smart."

Her cheeks pinked. "One of my foster moms did that and made a nice business out of it. I watched and learned."

He nodded and made a decision. He pulled her

toward the next corner cafe. "We need coffee and food for you if we're going to keep going. I had an early lunch."

"I didn't know you were a coffee person."

"I like the sweet stuff." He shrugged and pulled open the door to the café.

"But you're kind of a health nut, aren't you?"

He chuckled as they walked to the short line. "Not all the time. Come on. This is a big day for me. It's not everyday a man gets engaged." He winked and wiggled his ring hand in the air. "We'll go find yours after coffee. What would you like? My treat."

"Water and this salad." She handed him a very basic looking salad from the cooler.

"That's it?"

She nodded. "I hate tea and coffee, and I try to stay away from sweet drinks. That's the only gluten free salad here."

"Okay." He pushed away disappointment. How could he marry someone who hated coffee? He placed the order, and a few minutes later they were seated beside the window.

Katie guzzled down the water like a camel.

"You were thirsty."

She nodded. "There's something I need to ask you."

"Okay." The serious look on her face made him put down his mocha.

"You mentioned planning our wedding. I thought a simple ceremony down at the courthouse would be fine."

"I'm sure we can do better than that." His mother would take it as a personal offense if they married at the county courthouse. "My church is out, since we meet in a school. What about yours?"

She shook her head. "Not a chance. That place has stuff going on every night of the week. It books out a year in advance. I don't see how we could find anyplace at this late date. I've been helping Brandi plan their wedding, and there is no way we will be able to find a site for the ceremony, much less a florist, musicians, cake, and a caterer with our wedding so close. And who knows what else I'm forgetting."

"Hmm." He brought his cup to his mouth and took several sips of the drink. "I have an idea. It's a bit farfetched, but hear me out."

"Okay."

"How do you feel about boxing?"

"Like the sport?"

He chuckled. "Yes."

"I haven't given it any thought. Why?" Her brow puckered.

"We could get married in the boxing ring in the basement of The Ring and hold the reception at the community center."

A blank look met his gaze.

"Bad idea?" Disappointment struck him. Which was nuts since he'd never considered the idea before now.

"I guess I need to see it. I'm not a fan of basements in general. They tend to be so dark. On the other hand, it is kind of a fun idea. Would we wear normal wedding clothes?"

"Whatever you want."

She tilted her head to the side. Sunshine glinted off her golden hair. An inner light shone in her eyes.

Ray could see she was warming to the idea. "I'm sure I could get my pastor to officiate." He finished off his mocha. "You ready? I have to be back at the athletic club by one, so we should get a move on."

"Sure." She stood and followed after him. "Where are we going?"

"There's a jewelry store a couple blocks over." He adjusted his stride so she didn't have to jog to keep up with him. "How tall are you?"

"Five-foot-four inches. Why?"

"Just curious."

The next hour flew by in a blur. They hadn't found anything Katie would agree to. She declared everything too fancy or the stones too big. To which he replied engagement rings were supposed to be extra fancy—she wanted nothing to do with those rings. The only thing he managed to accomplish was learning her ring size—a six. He pulled the door open to The Ring Athletic Club. "Come with me downstairs. I want to show you the boxing ring." He waved to Tasha as they passed by the front desk then trotted down the stairs and stood with his hand in his pocket. "What do you think?"

Shell-shock covered her face. She glanced at him then at the ring. "Well, I guess I see potential. We could put flower arrangements at the four corners and an arbor in the center." She looked up at him. "But how would I get in there wearing a wedding gown?"

"Maybe you could pick out a dress without a long train."

She nodded as if contemplating the idea. Then she walked around the ring.

He realized for the first time all the men had stopped working out and were watching Katie's every move. A few flung curious looks at him. "Katie." He held his hand out to her.

She looked at it as if she had no idea what to do with it but moved toward him. He draped an arm across her shoulders. "As long we have everyone's attention. I'd like to introduce my fiancée. This is Katie."

Katie shot him a look that would silence most people then offered a smile and a wave to the guys. "I need to go," she said through the side of her mouth.

"Sorry for the interruption."

"When's the big day?" Rusty, the trainer who'd been on staff here forever, stood beside the ring holding a pair of boxing gloves.

"We haven't set the date yet. I'll let you know."

Katie rushed ahead of him and up the stairs. Then without even asking, she hustled to the staircase that led to his office and ran up that one, too.

He followed and closed the door after her. "You okay?"

"I don't know. That was weird." Her hands clutched the armrests of the same chair she sat in the last two times she'd been in his office.

"I'm sorry. I didn't mean to upset you." He eased

down onto the chair beside hers. "Do you feel like talking?"

She nodded. "You didn't upset me. I got overwhelmed. I do that sometimes. You'll get used to it."

He chuckled. "Okay." He sure hoped she didn't make a habit of rushing from rooms every time she got overwhelmed. "What do you think of my idea now that you've seen the ring?"

"It has promise." Her gaze shot to his. "Are we crazy?" Her eyes searched his.

He pressed his thumb and pointer finger together then pulled them slightly apart. "Maybe a little. Do you want to change your mind?"

"No. Not yet at least. Do you?"

He shook his head. This wedding may be an arrangement between them, but the more time he spent with *this* Katie, the more he was intrigued. He also knew the Lord had directed the agreement they had made. Even if he'd been uncertain he'd understood Him right and hadn't proposed to her in the first place, God didn't need him as it turned out since He nudged Katie too. Now to keep his wits about him and not mess anything up.

5

Thursday evening, Katie hauled another box down to the garage from the apartment above. Everything was happening so fast. She'd only become engaged to Ray this morning, and now she had a second job, a new apartment, and a fiancé.

"Remind me again why I agreed to help you with this." Brandi asked as she passed Katie on the stairs heading back up to the apartment.

She rolled her eyes. Brandi had given her nothing but grief since she picked up the first box and broke a fingernail. Katie left the box in the corner of the garage and slugged up the stairs. Truth was, this was much harder than she'd expected. When Ray said the place needed cleaning, he failed to mention he was a book hoarder. Too bad he wasn't here to help.

Brandi heaved the last box into her arms. "I can't believe Ray left all of these boxes here for you to move."

"Me neither," Katie mumbled. She stood in the center of the studio apartment and took in the space now that it was clear of boxes. To the right of the door, a kitchenette with a window that overlooked the driveway had a white Corian countertop and a stainless steel double sink. An apartment-sized refrigerator flanked the lone counter on the far left and a built in oven and stove combo to the right. The rear of the apartment looked like the best option for her bed. Maybe a couple of screens would give her a sense of division from the rest of the room. The center would be her combo dining and living space. Cozy.

Brandi tromped back inside and wiped the back of her hand across her forehead. "I know I've asked already, but are you sure about this?"

"You mean moving in here and being Emily's nanny?"

"Yes. Unless there's something you left out." She crossed her arms and raised a brow.

"Why would you ask me that?" She had deliberately left out the fact she and Ray were getting married. If Brandi was this concerned about her moving here to be a child's nanny, how would she react to a marriage of convenience? She didn't want her friend to do anything rash, like refuse to move to England to keep an eye on her. She wouldn't put it past Brandi either. Then again, her friend would find out sooner or later, and not telling her would have worse consequences than telling her. "You'd better sit."

Brandi looked around the space. "Where?"

"Good point." She took a bracing breath. "Ray and I are getting married."

"And you didn't tell me until now? So he decided to go through with it." Brandi shook her head as if in disbelief. "How long will you have to stay married to fulfill the conditions of the will?"

"Actually we're not planning to divorce. I like Ray, and I want to help him and Emily. They need me. And I think I need them, too."

"Whoa, this is such a shock. Who else knows?"

Katie shrugged. "The guys at the boxing ring. Other than that, I'm not sure. Everything is going so fast. We only decided to get married today and haven't set a date, but it'll have to be soon since Ray needs to be married before his birthday."

"I can't believe the guys at the boxing ring knew you were getting married before me," Brandi mumbled.

"That wasn't my doing. But I get how you feel."

Brandi crossed her arms. "I promise I won't ask this again, but are you sure about this? Marriage is a huge commitment."

"I agree. They need me." No one had ever needed her. "I want to marry Ray."

"Okay." Brandi's brow crinkled. "Ray's house isn't exactly on the bus line. You'll have to walk several blocks to get to a bus stop. I didn't say anything before because I thought you'd only be here a short time. It won't be fun in the pouring rain. That's the tip of the iceberg of my list on why this is a mistake. But if you're sure, there's nothing so big that can't be worked out with a little ingenuity."

"Agreed. Besides with the extra money I make

taking care of Emily, I could buy a car."

"Good. I won't worry about you as much if you have wheels." Brandi looked sincere. "I'm sorry I'm such a grump today. My best friend is moving out without warning, and I'm going to miss her wedding."

Katie shook her head. "Don't forget you started this by moving to England. It's not like I had a lot of choice. I had to move one way or the other." She waved a hand. "Let's make this shine before Ian and Ray get here with my stuff." They'd brought cleaning supplies with them. It wouldn't take too long to wash the three windows, vacuum the carpet, and clean the tiny bathroom near her sleeping area.

"Where's Emily?" Brandi asked.

"She's staying over at her grandmother's tonight and tomorrow. I'll officially start working here on Monday."

An hour later, the aroma of lemon filled her apartment, which no longer reeked of dust. Footsteps on the wooded stairs leading to the door alerted her to the guys' arrival. "They're here. We finished just in time."

"Good. While they move the big stuff in, you can direct them, and I'll go get pizza. I'm starving!"

"I only have a bed, a dresser, and a few boxes. Don't bother, we'll be finished in a few minutes, and you and Ian can go out together."

The guys walked inside.

Ray grinned. "This is the best the apartment has looked since I bought the place. I forgot how spacious it is."

Katie raised a brow at his description of spacious.

Without furniture the place looked big, but once she saved money to furnish it, that would change. Or would he want her to move into the house after they were married? Regardless, this space was very livable.

"Where should the bed and dresser go?"

Katie pointed to the back wall.

They deposited the bed then returned with Brandi's couch.

"That's not supposed to be here." Katie shot a panicked look toward her friend.

"I thought you could store it for me while I'm living in England. It makes more sense to leave the big stuff here. Do you mind?"

"No." She'd hoped to make this feel like her own, but it would be nice to have at least one piece of furniture to get her started, at least for now. Brandi and Ian were supposed to be in England for eighteen months. That would give her plenty of time to save money and plan how to decorate the space in her own taste, unless she ended up moving into Ray's house. That was a conversation for another time. "What about you? Where are you going to sit? Your wedding is still nine days away."

"I have the table and chairs. I'm giving those to my sister. She'll pick them up on Friday. You're actually doing us a favor by taking it."

"Okay. If you're happy, then I'm happy."

A short time later, Katie was completely moved in. "Thanks for the help." She walked her friends to the door, hugged Brandi, then Ian. "I'm going to miss you guys."

"We'll see you next Friday night at the wedding rehearsal if not sooner," Brandi said.

Katie nodded, not trusting her voice. For the first time since Ray proposed, the enormity of what she'd agreed to do hit her.

Ray hung back. "Can we talk?"

She nodded, turned, and eased onto the couch.

He sat in the opposite corner. "I've been doing some footwork regarding our wedding."

She cleared her throat. "And?"

"I've booked the boxing ring."

She laughed. "Sorry. You have no idea how ridiculous that sounds. I can't believe we're going to get married in a boxing ring."

"Why not? People get married in all kinds of places. Hot air balloons, under water—"

"Gardens, churches, courthouses." She grinned. "But your boxing ring is fine as long as the gloves are off."

He chuckled. "Promise. What do you think of the apartment?"

"I like it. Although you could have moved the boxes of books before we got here."

He smacked his forehead. "I completely forgot those were up here. I'm sorry. Were they a pain?"

"Oh, I'll feel them tomorrow."

He stood and walked around to the backside of the couch. Before she realized what he was doing, his hands were kneading her tired shoulders. "How's that?"

"Nice." She closed her eyes and allowed the tension and tiredness to melt away. "You're good at this."

"Thanks. We should talk about how things are going to play out over the next few months."

Relief surged though her. "That would be great. What's your plan?"

His touch on her shoulders lightened. "I was hoping we could work that out together." He stopped massaging her shoulders and returned to his seat on the couch.

"Okay. I vote for a small wedding. I won't be inviting anyone."

His eyes widened. "Why not? Are you ashamed to marry me?"

"What? No!"

"Then what's the problem? Why won't you invite any guests? Is it the cost? I'm paying, so don't worry about that."

She sighed. "Ray, you're one of the kindest men I have ever met. And you're incredibly good looking, and I enjoy being with you. So, no, I'm not ashamed to marry you."

Whoa! He had no idea Katie felt those things about him. He couldn't stop the grin that slid across his face.

"What?" Katie's cheeks pinked.

"I didn't know you felt that way about me. For the record, I feel the same about you. There aren't many women who'd marry a guy they didn't love simply to help him out. Of course, I hope that we'll love each other at some point." This had to be one of the most awkward conversations he'd ever had. But it was necessary if he ever hoped to have a true marriage with Katie.

"I agree. A loveless marriage would become a burden at some point and make us miserable. Plus, we have Emily to consider."

"Yes." His precious niece had had a rough time since her parents' death. He'd found a grief counselor to help her process and hoped the sessions would soon help. The poor child had cried herself to sleep every night since he'd told her about her parents. He swallowed the lump in his throat.

The couch shifted, and he turned toward Katie. She'd moved closer and tucked one leg under herself to face him on the cushion beside his. Concern filled her eyes. "Are you okay?" She reached for his hand.

He took hers in his and gave it a squeeze. "Yes, I was thinking about Emily. She's not doing all that well."

Katie nibbled on her bottom lip. "Kids are strong. I should know. She has a loving family, and that'll go a long way in aiding her."

"I'm so glad I have you to help me. I have no idea what I'd have done without you."

She pulled her hand away, and before he realized her intent, she had her arms wrapped around his neck. "It's going to be okay, Ray. Not today or tomorrow, but someday things will feel right again. Trust me. I know."

He had no idea what to do with his arms. If he hugged her back, she'd end up in his lap—not a bad thing, but probably a bad idea. He patted her back. "Thanks. Would you like to get breakfast with me in the morning? It's a Friday morning ritual."

She released him and sat back in her own space. "I'd like that. Thanks. It's been a long day. Do you mind if we finish this conversation another time?"

He stood. "That'll be fine. Although I warn you, once Emily is here, there will be little time to ourselves."

She nodded. "Before you go, I have one quick question." She laced her fingers in front of her and didn't make eye contact with him. "Once we're married, where will I be living?"

Like a punch to the gut, he let his breath out in a whoosh. "I hadn't thought that far ahead." At least not enough to come up with a concrete conclusion. "Where would you like to live?"

"I'm thinking that for Emily's sake I should move into the house. It's a three bedroom right?"

He nodded.

"Don't you think it will be difficult for her to understand why her aunt doesn't live with her uncle?" She tipped her head and caught his eyes.

"I guess we have a lot to consider. I'd like for our marriage to be a real marriage, but I don't want either of us to feel pressure."

"Sure. I understand." Her tone sounded distant as if he were suddenly a stranger. She strode past him and pulled open the door. "I'll see you tomorrow. Good night, Ray."

His shoulders sagged—clearly he hadn't handled

that as well as he should have. He paused in the doorway and looked toward her. She stood with her arms crossed. "Good night, Katie." With heavy feet, he trudged down the stairs to the driveway below. Unfortunately two steps forward and one step back seemed to be his norm with Katie. Somehow he had to do better. Maybe Ian had an idea.

He picked up his pace and slipped into his house via the kitchen door that was next to the garage. He pulled out his cell. One ring. Two.

"Hey, Ray. What's up? Did we forget to bring something over?"

"Not that I know of." It occurred to him, he hadn't told Ian about his engagement. "Funny thing, I forgot to mention something earlier."

"What's that?"

His neck heated. "Katie and I are getting married."

"You're kidding!" Ian chuckled. "I sure didn't see that coming—although now that I think about it, I should have. Are congratulations in order, or is this a marriage of convenience?"

"Ah, both?"

"Interesting." He sounded confused. "Maybe you better fill me in from the beginning."

Ray told him everything. "The thing is, I need Katie, and I can see us having a great life together. But I don't want to marry only a friend. I want to marry someone I love. I can't believe she's been there all along, and I didn't notice her."

Silence greeted him.

"You there, Ian?"

His buddy cleared his throat. "Uh. Yeah. I'm speechless. I thought you were a confirmed bachelor. So what do you need from me?"

"Advice. How do we fall in love?"

"You don't ask easy questions."

"If it was easy, I wouldn't have asked." He grinned, knowing his friend was likely doing the same.

"First off, love is a choice. Brandi and I did pre-marital counseling with our pastor, and that's something he hammered into us. He said that there will be days or weeks or months when we don't feel the love, and we must choose to love each other."

"Hmm. Okay. What else?" He'd never considered that love was a choice, but perhaps it was.

"You need to make each other a priority. She needs to know you care about her and vice versa. Make her feel special."

"Like with flowers?"

"That's a start. It doesn't have to be big. Brandi says it's the little things. Like remembering to clear my dishes when she has me over or putting the toilet seat down."

He chuckled. "Interesting. Okay. Anything else?"

"Pray together. Maybe even do devotions together."

His friend's words could not have surprised him more. Although they both went to church, they rarely, if ever spoke about spiritual things. Was he even capable of being that vulnerable? The idea of praying out loud and sharing his deepest thoughts with Katie knotted his stomach. He loved the Lord, but expressing himself in that way would not be easy. "Ah. Okay. I guess that's enough. Thanks."

"No problem. I'm sorry I'll miss the wedding." Ian groaned.

"What's wrong?"

"Brandi. When she finds out she won't be there for her best friend…Let's just say, it won't be pretty. I don't suppose you could move up your wedding so we'll be around?"

"Move it up? From what Katie says, what we're trying to do is nearly impossible as it is. There's no way we could pull off a wedding in a week."

"Yeah. I suppose you're right. Brandi's been going nuts with all the preparations. I'm sorry we won't be there. Hold on a minute. Brandi's trying to tell me something."

A moment later, his buddy laughed.

"Hey, what's going on over there?" Ray asked.

"Sorry. It appears Brandi already knows about the wedding. And I was right. She's not happy about missing it."

"It won't be the same without my best man." Were they doing the right thing to wait? Maybe they should get married right away, but Katie wanted him to get to know her. He could hear Brandi talking to Ian. "Sounds like you're busy. I'll let you go." He set his phone on the kitchen counter then walked to the kitchen window and glanced up at the apartment above the garage. Should he suggest moving up the wedding? Katie had been upset Brandi wouldn't be there, too, but he wasn't sure he was ready to sign on the dotted line, so to speak, so fast.

6

Friday morning, Ray met Katie in the driveway. "Good morning."

"Hey." She yawned and swayed slightly then blinked.

"You okay?" He grasped her arm to steady her.

"I'm ready to drop. I've never lived alone, and every little sound startled me. I think I finally fell asleep an hour before my alarm went off."

"Ouch. We don't have to get breakfast." Did she want to marry him so she wouldn't have to be alone? No way. Though young, she was independent. That couldn't be a reason.

"No. I want to. I love going out to eat. I hope they have gluten free options though."

"That's right. I keep forgetting about that. I'm sure you'll be able to find something."

"I hope you're right, but I'll be fine with a cup of coffee."

"I thought you didn't drink coffee."

"I don't, but this is an extenuating circumstance. I'll gag it down for the caffeine infusion I constantly hear about from Brandi."

He chuckled. "You could always get a soda."

She wrinkled her nose. "I can't stand the stuff. It tastes like metal. I'd rather have one of those sweet coffee drinks everyone is addicted to."

"Works for me. It's nice to have you on the dark side with the rest of us." Ray opened the door to his Honda for her, then closed it and strode to his side. He settled into his seat then backed out of the driveway. She was going to love his go-to breakfast joint. "I know you didn't sleep well, but I'm curious if you're a morning person or not?"

"Not." She stretched like a cat. "How far away is this place?"

"Not far. It's in the Capitol Hill neighborhood. You're going to love it. It's a true coffee shop, and the food is amazing. I eat there every Friday morning, but sometimes there's a long wait since the place is small."

She chuckled. "Your favorite place is a coffee shop, and I don't like coffee. How is it we're engaged?" She shot him a wry grin.

"I asked myself that same question." It was nice to see this relaxed version of Katie. She was kind of funny when loopy.

"You look nice today. What's with the khaki pants and button up? Don't get me wrong. I like the look, but it's not your norm."

He glanced down at his checked shirt. "Thanks. I

suppose you're accustomed to seeing me in athletic wear. We have an appointment with my grandfather's attorney after breakfast. I see you're in your standard coat and jeans."

"You don't like my coat?" Hurt filled her voice.

He shrugged. "I have no opinion one way or the other. It was only a random comment. Sorry, I didn't mean to offend you."

"You didn't. I suppose I wear it too often. My foster mom, the last one I had, once told me if I wore a nice coat over my clothes no one would notice what was underneath."

"Was there something wrong with what you wore?"

She shrugged. "I didn't have nice clothes, but I was given a super nice coat from a charity for foster kids, and I wore it until it got ruined. When I graduated from high school, my foster parents threw me a party where I received a bunch of money, and I bought this." She ran her hand along the sleeve of her jacket. "I found it at a consignment shop. It was my one and only splurge on myself."

"Thanks for telling me that story. I imagine it wasn't easy being in the system." So much about Katie's quirks fell into place now.

"You're right, but if we're going to marry, there are things you should know about me."

He felt her gaze upon him and glanced her way. "There's more?" The intensity on her face almost seared him.

"Nothing much, but I can be moody. I want to go

back to college, and I enjoy musical theater." She shifted in her seat. "I'm putting a lot of trust in you. I like to think I'm a good judge of character and that you're a good risk."

"You can trust me, Katie."

She nodded. "Now you need to trust me."

He jerked his head in her direction. "What's that supposed to mean?"

"Eyes on the road," her voice rose a notch.

He slammed on the brake at a red light. "Sorry. What did you mean when you said I need to trust you?"

"You must be hurting after Renee's and Matt's deaths, and then you've been thrust into being a dad, and now you saddled yourself with me. You're a rock, Ray. But you can talk to me. I can keep my mouth shut."

He blinked. A car horn honked. He pulled forward. It was a good thing the restaurant was up ahead, or they might not get there in one piece. He shuddered at the thought. "Thank you. I might take you up on that but not now." He pulled along the curb and parked.

"Works for me, so long as you do at some point."

How did he not know Katie was so sweet and bold, too? Sure Brandi thought the world of her, but his fiancée had never allowed him to get to know her until that night at the diner. What had changed for her to open up and show her true self?

She hopped out of the car without waiting for him to open the door. "This place looks comfortable."

He grinned. "That's a perfect description." He rested a hand on her back as they went into the bustling diner. After waiting for a table for fifteen minutes, they were seated by a window. A short time later they placed their order.

"I talked with Ian last night. He pointed out how close you and Brandi are."

"You should've known that already."

"I suppose you're right. Are you sure it'll be okay to not have her at your wedding?"

"It's fine."

"But you won't have anyone there with you. Won't you need help with your dress and hair and stuff?"

She giggled and ran a hand through her short hair. "Um, I think I can handle it. It's pretty easy. As for the dress, I still need to figure that out."

"We could play hooky today and go wedding dress shopping."

"That sounds like fun. I do want Brandi at my wedding, but I don't see how it's possible."

"It is if we get married before they leave."

"Impossible. Plus your sister died recently—won't people talk if you get married so soon after?"

"Let them talk. I don't care."

"What about your mom. She's kind of…"

"Uptight. Prim and proper. Straight laced." He loved how Katie's eyes twinkled at the description of his mother.

"Don't forget regal, beautiful, and she loves you."

Leave it to Katie to point that out. "I want you to have someone you care about at our wedding. Let's get married before Brandi and Ian leave."

"Let me think about it while we eat. Speaking of which…"

The waitress delivered their meals.

Ray's heart pounded. Why had he suggested they get married so soon? What if she felt pressured and changed her mind. He sure felt the pressure. But it would be a lot easier if they married sooner than later, for so many reasons.

Katie ate her scrambled eggs in silence, giving him no clue to her thoughts.

Ray grabbed his gym bag with workout clothes and boxing gloves inside then went downstairs. He needed to burn off some stress. He'd enjoyed sharing breakfast with Katie until he'd brought up getting married next week. Then things changed. She hadn't said much since, only that she needed to take a walk to think—probably a good idea. He needed thinking time, too.

"Everything okay, boss?" Tasha asked as he strode past the reception desk at the bottom of the stairs. "Your fiancée sure left in a hurry."

"She's taking a walk. When she gets back, please have her wait in my office. I'll be downstairs." He headed to the basement where the boxing ring was housed along with several bags that hung on one side of the space—the basement ring and boxing equipment, the only throwback to another era for which the athletic club was named.

He waved to a couple of regulars as he made his

way into the tiny locker room. He quickly changed and found the trainer to help with his gloves.

Rusty eyed him. "You okay? It's not like you to come down here in the morning."

"I've been better. How're things?"

"Same as always." Translation, the regulars were still coming in, and he had nothing new to report. The grizzled trainer helped him with the gloves then accompanied him to his favorite punching bag.

Ray jabbed at the bag and soon found a rhythm—right hook, left hook…Thirty minutes later, sweat trickled down his back. "I'm done."

"Feel better?" Rusty worked to pull off a glove.

"Some." What he felt was sore and tired. It'd been a long time since he'd pushed himself like that.

Rusty chuckled. "If I didn't know better, I'd say you were having woman troubles."

"Something like that. Were you ever married, Rusty?" He pulled off the other glove.

"I was. Thirty-five years with my sweetheart. We had our ups and downs, but we were always there for each other."

"Hopefully more ups than downs."

He nodded. "Yep. Your granddad and I went way back. I know the two of you were close. If you ever need to talk…"

Ray swallowed the sudden lump in his throat. "Thanks. I'll keep that in mind. You were a good friend to Gramps."

"And he to me. I'm here anytime, Ray."

Ray clapped him on the shoulder. "You're the best. I checked the calendar and the ring looks free Thursday evening. It's not a for sure thing yet, but is there any reason that you know of that would prevent Katie and me from having the wedding here in the ring that night?"

Rusty chuckled, revealing a toothy grin. "Your bride okay with a quickie wedding in a boxing ring?"

He shrugged. "That's what I'm waiting to find out."

Rusty nodded. "The ring is open. I'll remove the ropes on one side and get it ready for you if it's a go." He chuckled again. "She must be some woman to be willing to get married down here."

"She is. Thanks." Relief surged through him. Now that Rusty was behind him, he knew this would go smoothly. "I'd better hit the shower. Take it easy." He refused to worry any longer if Katie would back out of marrying him. The Lord had been clear that he was to propose, but then when he'd gotten cold feet, she'd proposed to him. Clearly, marriage was God's plan for them.

Moving up the timeline was a stressor, but Katie deserved to have her best friend there. It was important for her to have someone at their wedding she could lean on. Even though he believed their marriage was God ordained, he wasn't kidding himself that things would be perfect. Life was messy, as he knew all too well.

Katie sat in Ray's office at the athletic club. She must be experiencing some kind of mental breakdown from lack of sleep. She needed to talk to Brandi, but first she needed to let Ray know the wedding was on.

The office door opened, and Ray sauntered in, closing it behind him.

She stood to face him, taking in his wet hair and fresh clean scent—nice.

He tilted his head and met her eyes. "Assuming you're onboard, we're all set for next Thursday night. We can use the boxing ring for the wedding and the community center for the reception."

Her stomach dropped. "We're really doing this?" Her legs weakened, and she grasped the back of the chair. Somehow, she didn't think he'd be able to make it work. Her heart pounded, and her pulse thrummed loudly in her ears. She blinked back sudden tears. "Everything is happening so fast. I hate to admit it, but I'm scared" She looked at him through watery eyes. A tear escaped. She swiped it away. Should she tell Ray that the day he'd cleared was her birthday?

No. She wasn't much for celebrating the day, never taking much note of it herself.

"Oh, Katie. I'm sorry." He stepped closer to her and placed a gentle hand on her shoulder. "We can slow things down. Don't cry."

She stood, stepped into his arms, and closed her eyes as she wrapped her arms around his waist.

He held her. "It'll be okay. We can stick with our original plan, if we're moving too fast."

His sweet concern and willingness to change touched her deeply. No man had ever tried so hard or cared so much about her feelings. Resolve strengthened her. She tilted her head back. "I'll marry you on Thursday. I was overwhelmed for a moment by how fast things are happening, but I'm fine now. Thursday works."

"It does?" His face brightened. "You will?"

She nodded and sniffed. "I'm sorry for losing it on you. But you may as well know, I cry sometimes when I'm overly tired and stressed. I try not to, but it happens."

He dropped a kiss on her forehead. "It's fine. I think it's normal for a bride to get emotional. And I know how tired you are." He rubbed her back gently. "You going to be okay?"

She nodded. It felt so good to be held by Ray, but the gesture wasn't a romantic one—he was only trying to comfort her. She dropped her arms and stepped back.

"I have tissues around here someplace." He spun around and pulled open a cupboard then handed her a box of tissues.

"Thank you." She dried her eyes and blew her nose.

He looked at her with uncertainty in his gaze. "You're okay now? Really?"

She nodded, feeling her face grow hot. "Emily will be home tonight, so I need to find a dress today. I don't imagine wedding dress shopping with a four-year-old would be much fun."

"I'll take you right now. Let me buy your dress. You're doing this for me, and don't think for a minute I don't understand the sacrifice you're making."

"Thank you," she said softly. Marrying him was not a huge sacrifice. She was already halfway in love with him.

"I'm assuming, based on what you've already said, there's no one you'd like to join us."

She nodded. It wasn't like she had a mom or sister to go dress shopping with, or anyone who'd care besides Brandi, and her friend was too busy to bother right now. Katie caught her breath. "I need to make sure Brandi will be able to make it to the wedding." Her eyes widened, and her gaze shot to his. "What if they have plans?"

"I already checked with Ian. He said they'd be there."

"What about flowers and cake and all the other stuff?"

"I talked to my little sister, Hailey, a bit ago—she's up for the challenge. Mind you, everything will be simple. I'm only inviting close friends and family."

She took a breath and let it out slowly. "That all sounds great." The only person she cared to invite was Brandi. Sure she had a few church friends, but no one close enough she cared to explain her situation to. It was such a relief knowing the friend who was like a sister to her would be there. Ray was truly a thoughtful man. This had to be difficult on him. She blinked her watery eyes, hoping they wouldn't overflow again. "We should get a move on." Breakfast and their meeting at the attorney's office had eaten up a good chunk of the morning. She still wanted to laugh when she thought about the attorney's face when Ray introduced her as his fiancée.

The man looked astounded that Ray was engaged and that he would fulfill the requirement of the will. He'd stuttered for several seconds before getting himself under control and congratulating them.

Ray wrapped his hand around hers. "Let's go get you a dress. Where to?"

"I don't know. A thrift shop?"

"No. There won't be time to have it dry-cleaned."

"Oh." She'd never had anything dry-cleaned and had no idea if he was correct, but she wouldn't argue. "Then where?"

"I guess we can try some bridal gown shops. There's bound to be a store with an appropriate dress."

They spent the rest of the day shopping, but by the end she was ready to give up. Who would have thought finding a wedding dress off the rack would be so difficult? They were either too long, or too short, too tight, or too big in all the wrong places.

"We need to change our strategy," Ray said. "How about if you pick out a white dress that you like. It doesn't need to be a traditional wedding dress."

"Are you sure?"

He nodded. "Let's find a Nordwear. My mom loves shopping there, so they must be a decent place to look because she's picky."

"Sounds good to me." She hadn't considered not wearing a wedding dress, but this wasn't going to be a traditional marriage, so there was no need to wear a traditional gown. At this point she'd prefer to wear something from her closet, but she didn't want to disappoint Ray.

They headed to the nearest Nordwear and went inside.

"I'll be at the café. Text me when you're ready."

She wandered around the store for a while and finally found the right department. A saleswoman approached her, and Katie explained her mission.

"I have a few dresses that might work."

Katie followed the woman to a rack where she pulled a scalloped, fitted on top and flared on the bottom dress off the rack. Katie caught her breath. "That's the one." She took it to the dressing room and changed.

"When you get it on, come out and show me," the saleswoman said.

Katie pulled the door open and stepped out.

"Very nice. Turn."

Katie did as she requested and noticed a three-way mirror at the end of the room. She walked over to it and stepped up onto the platform. The dress hit mid-calf and was a perfect fit. She couldn't stop smiling. "I'll take it!"

"Wonderful. What about shoes?"

"Hmm. What do you suggest? I'm not used to heels? And we're getting married in a boxing ring."

A smile lit the woman's face. "That's unique. You could do white pumps. Or if you want to break all the rules why not wear white, lacy sneakers?"

Now that was the best idea ever. She'd have to find a pair and fast. Ray had been wilting on her before she came in here, and she wasn't doing a whole lot better.

She went back to the dressing room, sent him a text where to meet her to pay and then changed as quickly as she could. Traditional wedding or not, she wanted her dress to be a surprise.

She managed to beat him to the register, and the woman happily hid it in a dress bag for her. She waved to Ray when she spotted him.

"You found one?"

"I did, but you can't see it."

He raised a brow and grinned. "Why's that?"

"I want it to be a surprise."

"Fair enough." He quickly paid. "What next?" He handed her a covered cup. "I bought you a vanilla latte since you seemed to not hate the coffee you had at breakfast. I did a quick Google search, and it appears to be gluten free."

Her heart warmed. "That was thoughtful. Thanks." She sipped the sweet drink.

"I think you'll like it a lot more than plain coffee and figured you could use a pick-me-up by now. Oh, and this, too." He pulled a little bag from his jacket pocket. "It's a gluten free muffin."

"Seriously?" She looked inside the bag. Hopefully it would taste as good as it looked. "Thanks. What about you?"

"I had a snack at the café while waiting."

"Okay." She sipped the coffee. He was right; she didn't hate it, and it was much better than the plain sugar-sweetened coffee she'd ordered at breakfast. She wouldn't take up the habit of coffee, though. It was more of a necessary evil to keep her body and mind moving. "Thanks for today, Ray."

"Why are you thanking me? Seems all I've done is complicate your life."

She took a bite of the chocolate muffin and savored the deliciousness of having a party in her mouth. This was better than she'd expected.

He chuckled. "Remind me to never come between you and food. Speaking of which, I was thinking we'd keep it simple and only serve cake and punch at our reception."

"Whatever you want. Do we have a photographer?"

"Yes. Kari's not a pro, but she could be."

"Okay." She couldn't help the feeling of disappointment that hit her. Although she may never have dreamed of a fairytale wedding, she didn't want it to be an afterthought either. It was too late now, though. She'd given her word, and she wouldn't take it back.

7

Katie stood beside Ray as they waited for his mother to retrieve Emily from the TV room. On tiptoe, she spoke into his ear. "It sounds like she's been watching television since she's been here."

"Except to sleep, I think you're right. My mom was never a hands-on parent. She preferred to let others do the job." He kept his voice low. "I wonder where Hailey is? I thought she might pitch in and help with Emily."

His minty breath tickled her nose, and she sneezed.

"Bless you." He draped his arm across her shoulder.

"Thanks."

"Uncle Ray!" Emily skipped toward them across the travertine tile. "Katie!" She slid to a stop in her socks then wrapped her arms around Ray's leg. "I missed you."

He reached down and pulled her into his arms. "I missed you, too, squirt." He gave her a squeeze then shifted her to his side.

Mrs. O'Brien handed Ray a backpack. "She's eaten and had a bath."

"Thanks, Mom." Ray swung the bag onto his free shoulder.

Mrs. O'Brien nodded. "Will there be a rehearsal and dinner for your wedding? If you ask me, it's indecent to throw such a sacred event together as if it's no more special than a birthday party." She frowned. "I suppose I shouldn't expect more considering who you're marrying."

Katie's jaw dropped, but she quickly closed it. She should have expected a comment like that from this woman—a snob in every sense of the word.

"I hadn't thought about it," Ray said. "And I'd appreciate it if you'd show a little restraint and respect toward my fiancée."

Mrs. O'Brien grimaced. "Whoever heard of getting married in a boxing ring?" She shook her head. "But it's impossible to find a decent venue at this late date—I tried."

"The boxing ring was Grandpa's pride and joy. I'd think you'd like the idea."

She rolled her eyes. "I've never been one for sentimentalities." Her soon-to-be mother-in-law waved Ray's comment away as if it didn't matter, placed a kiss on his cheek, and then one on Emily's. "I guess I'll see you at the wedding. What are you doing with Emily on your wedding night? I assume you'll be going on a honeymoon."

"We aren't going anywhere right now. Ian and Brandi's wedding is Saturday afternoon so we'll be busy."

A smile brightened her eyes. "They're such a lovely

couple."

Katie slipped her hand into Ray's. His mother was awful. She hoped it was the stress and grief of losing her daughter that caused her rotten attitude. "We should get going. Emily needs to be in bed by eight."

"Right. Say good-bye to Grandma."

Emily tucked her head under Ray's chin. "Bye, bye." She waved then plopped her thumb into her mouth.

Katie frowned. When had that started? She'd never seen Emily suck her thumb.

They walked out to Ray's car together. He released her hand to palm his keys and unlock the car. "Here we go." He set his niece on the backseat. "Get into your booster and buckle up."

She quickly did as he requested. "Are you coming with us to Uncle Ray's, Katie?" She plopped her thumb back into her mouth.

"Yes. I live in the garage apartment."

Emily's eyes lit up, and she pulled her thumb out of her mouth. "Goodie."

Ray started the car and headed in the direction of his house. "Katie is going to be taking care of you while I'm at work. What do you think of that?"

"Katie is fun." She giggled then quieted.

After a while, Katie looked over her shoulder. Emily's head rested back, with her thumb no longer in her mouth. She looked to be sound asleep. A state she hoped to be in soon, as well. She glanced toward Ray. He slouched, and he drove the speed limit. It'd been a long day, and it appeared to have gotten to Ray as well. "She's out."

"Good. Hopefully, she'll stay that way. I hate seeing her cry herself to sleep."

"Yeah." Katie had done that a lot after her mom left and then later when she'd been placed into foster care. She'd been one angry and hurt kid. It was no wonder she'd been sent from one home to another. No one knew how to deal with her rage. It took Brandi's friendship to start the healing process. When Brandi had invited her to visit the youth group at her church, she was hesitant to say yes but was glad she had. The years that followed were some of the best of her life.

Ray pulled into his driveway and parked in the garage. "I'll carry her in. Will you bring her bag?" he kept his voice low.

"Sure." She followed the duo to Emily's bedroom and placed the bag on top of the dresser. The stark white walls and plain blue comforter on the bed said bachelor, not little girl. She'd have to remedy that soon. Maybe she could get him to bring Emily's bedding here. It would make her feel more at home, and maybe she'd sleep easier, too.

Ray placed his niece into her bed and drew the sheet up to her chin. He flipped on a nightlight then pulled the door almost closed behind them. In the hall he touched a finger to his lips and motioned for her to follow.

Curious, she did.

He walked several feet to the end of the hall where it split into a T. He went left down a short hall, opened a door, and motioned for her to follow him inside.

She hesitated at the doorway. "Why are we in here?"

"I wanted to show you the bedroom you'll have after we're married—that is, if you still think it's a good idea to move in."

"I do, but I didn't realize you agreed."

He waved a hand motioning for her to enter. "You're welcome to redecorate."

"Thank you." She stepped into the medium-sized bedroom. These walls were white as well. "A little color on the walls might be nice. Nothing too crazy." A queen-sized bed with a white down comforter occupied the center of the main wall. Another door led to a Jack-and-Jill bathroom. She looked through the room and noted the door to the bedroom on the other end of the bathroom was closed. A white-washed chest of drawers sat opposite the bed, and a wing-backed chair occupied the corner of the room with a standing lamp beside it. "It's cozy. So you don't mind if I paint?"

"Not at all. I'm no decorator. The previous owners did everything in white. I spend most of my time at The Ring or the community center, so painting hasn't been a priority."

Her gaze shot to his face. "You go to the community center? I've never seen you there."

A resigned look crossed his face. He sat on the edge of the bed and patted the space beside him. "Come sit."

She didn't move.

"I don't bite, Katie. Surely, you know that by now." Hurt shone in his eyes.

She didn't mean to wound him, but trust was tough.

Especially when she'd spent much of her life trying to avoid potentially dangerous situations. But if she couldn't trust Ray, then there was no one she could trust. "You're right. I'm sorry." She settled beside him.

"Thank you. I need to tell you something that only a handful of people know. But you must promise that what I'm about to say won't leave this room."

"Okay." She nodded, not sure she wanted to hear but anxious to know his secret.

"When I took over running The Ring, I set up a foundation that directly funnels all profits above and beyond operating expenses including wages into the community center. The Ring makes it possible. Without that support the center would close."

She reminded herself to breathe. "I did not expect that." He was her benefactor in more ways than one.

"Good. I hope you understand this is confidential. No one can know, not even Brandi."

"I promise." She wrapped her arms around his bicep and hugged it. "You're a good man, Ray O'Brien, and I'm glad I'm marrying you." She released his arm and stood. Without looking back she traipsed from the room and fled the house to the privacy of her apartment. Could Ray really be as good as he seemed? A niggling doubt tickled the back of her mind.

Late Monday morning, Katie loaded the roller with lavender paint and slid it up and down a wall in Emily's room. "What do you think, Emily? Is it pretty?"

She replied, but the thumb in her mouth made it difficult to understand.

"I can't understand you when your mouth is full." She'd decided not to make an issue of the thumb sucking but refused to let her get away with it while talking.

The child's brow furrowed. She plucked her thumb from her mouth. "I like it." She hugged her doll with both arms. "Mommy's favorite color is purple."

Katie swallowed the sudden lump in her throat and plastered on a smile. "Your mommy had good taste. How do you like having the stuff from your bedroom here?"

She squeezed her doll tighter. "Good."

Katie turned back to the wall and continued to roll on the color. If she kept moving, she might finish before Emily lost interest and got antsy. Ray had moved all of Emily's belongings from her parents' house to here. When she'd asked, he didn't even hesitate and seemed chagrined to have not thought of it himself.

"Katie?"

"Yes?"

"I want my mommy."

She turned, faced her soon-to-be niece, and set the roller in the paint tray. "I'm sorry about your mommy. I know you miss her a lot. I miss mine, also."

"Your mommy died, too?"

She shook her head and sat, placing the roller in the tray. "No. Mine left me when I was a young girl. I guess she didn't want to be my mom anymore." Otherwise, she would have taken her away from her awful dad when she took off.

Emily crawled over to her then plopped into her lap. She snuggled close. Katie wrapped her arms around the little girl. "Your mommy loved you so much. She never would have left you on purpose."

"I know." Emily shifted and patted Katie's cheeks. "My mommy loved you, too. Do you have a daddy?"

Her stomach knotted. "I do. But he did something very bad, and he's in prison."

Her eyes widened. "When I'm bad, I have to go to my room."

Katie grinned at Emily's refreshing innocence. "When we do something wrong, we get punished."

She nodded with wide eyes. "Can I go watch TV?"

Katie looked around the room and spotted coloring books on a shelf. "How about you color while I paint?"

"Okay." The TV request as good as forgotten, Emily hopped up and got to work coloring.

Katie painted as quickly as she could without making a mess. With one wall completed, she stood back to see her work.

"Looks nice."

Katie screamed and nearly tossed the roller in the air. "Ray! What are you doing here?"

He chuckled.

"Uncle Ray!" Emily ran toward him and launched herself into his arms. "We're coloring."

"I see that." He winked at Katie.

Her face heated. Is this what it would be like to be a family? Warmth filled her from head to toe. "I thought you were working."

"I was, but I forgot something."

"What?"

"My lunch." He held up the bag she'd placed in the fridge earlier when he'd walked out without it.

"You could've eaten out, like usual."

"But then I would have missed this. Plus, I thought I'd give the two of you a ride to the community center."

"Oh. Thanks. What time is it?"

"Twelve thirty. We have plenty of time." He looked at her like she had two noses. "You umm…" He flicked his nose. "Have a little paint on your face."

"I've been so careful." She peered into the mirror above Emily's dresser and sighed. She must have touched her face with her hand. A smear down the side of her nose stood out against her pale skin. It had better come off easily. The last thing she wanted was lavender colored splotches on her face. "Maybe I should save painting until after the wedding."

"You're going to be my aunt, too." Emily patted her cheek from her perch in Ray's arms. "Aunt Hailey told me."

"That's right, sweetie. I can't wait. I've always wanted to be an aunt." She grinned at the little girl who'd captured her heart the first time they'd met.

Ray cleared his throat and set Emily on the floor. "If you want to finish painting after the wedding, it's fine with me." He looked at the wall she'd finished and nodded. "It looks nice. In fact, I wonder if that wall is the only one that needs color. It's the wall her bed's on, and it looks like a feature wall as is."

Katie stepped over to see it from his vantage point. "You're right. What do you think, Emily? Should all the walls be lavender or should we stick with one?"

Her face grew serious. "Will you paint that wall pink?" She pointed to the wall with her dresser. "And that one yellow." She pointed to the one with her shelves and toys. "And that one…" She frowned. Then her face lit. "Orange!"

Ray chuckled. "You want a rainbow room, huh?"

"Don't give her any ideas," Katie said through the side of her mouth.

Emily jumped up and down. "A rainbow! A rainbow!" She squealed. "Like Noah and the ark. We learned about Noah in Sunday school."

Katie couldn't help grinning. She didn't want to buy all the colors of the rainbow and paint one, but she couldn't say no to this precious little girl after what she'd been through. "How about a small one over your bed?" She liked Ray's idea of leaving the rest of the walls white, but doubted that would appease Emily.

"Maybe," Emily hedged. "I'm going to ballet class, Uncle Ray."

"Are you now?" He sent a knowing look toward Katie.

She caught her breath. His twinkling eyes crinkled ever so slightly. Seeing him happy was nice. His gaze connected with hers and held a moment before he shifted his attention to his niece.

"How about we all have lunch together downstairs."

He hoisted Emily into his arms without waiting for a reply and left the room.

Katie poured the remaining paint from the tray back into the can, pounded the lid on, then headed downstairs. She'd put plastic wrap around the roller and place it in the fridge—it would be moist and ready to go the next time she painted.

"What's for lunch?" Ray asked as he sliced up an apple.

She flicked on the water and scrubbed at her hands and arms. "Peanut butter and jelly for Emily. I'll do peanut butter and apple slices." She motioned toward the sack he'd placed on the counter. "I made you a nice lunch."

"I know. And I plan to enjoy it." He slid a plate of sliced apples to the middle of the counter. "Help yourselves."

Katie handed a slice to Emily.

Ray pulled bread from the cupboard and began making Emily's sandwich.

"You don't have to do that."

"I know. But you're busy enough, and I enjoy company while I'm eating. This way we can all eat together."

"You're the boss." She filled three cups with water. Her phone rang. "Hello?" Her stomach knotted as she listened to the familiar voice on the other end.

This couldn't be happening.

8

Ray tried to eavesdrop on Katie's conversation, but his niece hummed a song rising in volume with each note. He finally gave up and hummed along with Emily. Katie's comment about him being the boss bothered him. He didn't want her to think of him like that. They were partners, but he wouldn't correct her in front of Emily. Somehow, he had to romance his soon-to-be wife with his niece in tow.

He placed the top onto the sandwich and sliced it at an angle into fourths then placed it on a plate.

Katie pocketed her phone.

"Everything okay?"

"Sure." She stood erect. Her gaze darted toward the door.

He brought the plate to the table and sat beside Emily who'd already seated herself. "Aren't you going to sit, Katie?"

"Of course." She grinned, but the smile didn't reach her fear-filled eyes. She scooped peanut butter onto an apple wedge then plopped it into her mouth.

He chuckled. How could that tiny mouth fit all of that? "I'm impressed."

She shrugged then washed it down with a gulp of water. "It's a gift."

"I want to try." Emily brought a quarter of her BP&J to her mouth and opened wide and pushed. She pulled it away. "It won't fit."

Ray and Katie laughed together. Something stirred in Ray at the sound of their combined laughter. As unconventional as their arrangement was, he knew in his heart marrying Katie was right. He bit into the cold-cut sandwich Katie had prepared earlier for him—he could definitely get used to this. But he was concerned about Katie. Even though she'd joined him in laughter, she looked ready to bolt. What had that phone call been about?

A quick glance at the oven clock reminded him why he never came home for lunch—not enough time. "I hate to eat and run, but I need to get back. How fast can the two of you be ready to leave?"

Katie frowned. She looked down at herself and shook her head. "I think Emily and I will stay here until I need to leave for work."

"Are you sure?"

"Positive. I don't want to make you late." Katie motioned toward his lunch. "You didn't finish."

"I'll eat on the way." He placed a kiss on her cheek. "Thanks." His eyes met her surprised ones, and a sudden thought struck him. "I should've asked sooner, but my sister is meeting me at the club to discuss wedding plans. Would you like to come along?" He willed her to say yes. Maybe he'd be able to find out about her conversation on the way to the athletic club. "I can spare a few minutes for you to get cleaned up. I'll give Hailey a call and put her off a little. If you're taking the bus you'd need to leave soon anyway."

She bit her bottom lip. "I suppose you're right. Will you watch Emily while I get cleaned up?"

"Of course, but hurry."

She darted out the door.

Emily looked at him with doe eyes. "I love Katie, Uncle Ray."

He picked her up and carried her to the sink. "Let's get you washed up."

"Do you love Katie?" She squirted soap onto her hands, rubbed them together, then rinsed them.

"I like her a lot. I'm glad you love her. I think she loves you, too."

Emily giggled. "She said so."

"Good." He wouldn't lie about his feelings for Katie to appease his niece and was thankful she hadn't pushed the issue any more. "How about you go grab the bag Katie packed for you, and we'll wait in the car for her?"

"Okay." She darted from the room.

He shot off a quick text to Hailey, letting her know he would be late.

"Ready!" Emily wore a pink princess backpack.

"Let's go then." He led the way and locked up after them.

Katie rushed down the stairs from the apartment as they were walking to the car.

"That was fast." How could she possibly have gotten ready so quickly? He looked her over from head to toe. Her freshly scrubbed face looked virtually makeup free with no sign of the purple paint from earlier. Her jeans and red T-shirt took him aback. "Where's your jacket?" He'd grown accustomed to the ever-present part of her wardrobe.

"It's a nice day. I don't need it."

"True." Seattle had been experiencing an unusually dry spring.

Emily hummed a random tune from the backseat. He tried a couple of times to start a conversation with Katie but couldn't think of anything that didn't require more than a yes or no answer. Twenty minutes later, he pulled into his parking spot in the alley behind the athletic club. "Let's go upstairs and hear what Hailey's planning for our wedding."

She shook her head. An uneasy look crossed her face. "I've changed my mind. I trust your judgment. It'd be best if Emily and I head over to the community center."

"Are you sure?" Disappointment filled him. Why wouldn't she want to hear what his sister was planning? After all, the wedding was Katie's, too. Weren't the women supposed to care a lot about the cake and stuff? Or maybe this was about that phone call. He'd never found the right words to bring it up on the drive over. Now he'd have to try this evening.

Katie helped Emily from the car. "I'm sure." She lowered her voice. "I have things to do before the kids get there. Besides I think it'd be best to keep Emily away from your sister as much as possible. I know we don't always have a choice, but Hailey and Renee look so much alike, I'm afraid it might make things more difficult for her."

"That's ridiculous."

She stopped moving and looked at him for only a moment before shifting her gaze. "Maybe, but are you willing to risk that I'm right and you're wrong?"

What if being with Hailey was healing for his niece? Regardless, either way, it wouldn't hurt to send Emily with Katie. "Fine. I'll be by this evening to pick you up." He pulled the backdoor to the club open. "After you."

"Thanks." She rushed inside. Emily held tight to her hand. "Say good-bye to your uncle, Emily."

The child dropped her hold on Katie and quickly hugged his leg. "Can we come see you later?"

"Anytime, squirt. But remember Katie has to work, so only when she says it's okay."

Emily nodded. "Bye-bye."

He watched as Katie and his niece breezed past the reception desk and out the front entrance. Somehow, he didn't buy Katie's reasoning for leaving so fast. Could she be the one uncomfortable with his little sister? But why? It didn't make any sense. He headed up to his office and discovered Hailey sitting at a cluttered card table. "Sorry to keep you waiting."

"It's fine. I was almost here when I got your text."

Yikes! "You've been waiting awhile. I'm extra sorry."

She shrugged. "No problem. I'm about finished." She focused on something in front of her, so rather than bother her, he sat behind his desk and got to work checking e-mails.

Thirty minutes later, Ray looked up from the computer screen in his office. "Are we going to make it in time?"

"Yes, but I don't understand why you couldn't wait a month," Hailey said. "Pulling off a wedding this fast is next to impossible."

He sighed. "But we did it, and now Katie's best friend will be there. If we'd waited even a week longer, Brandi would be gone."

Hailey smiled. "You're sweet to consider your bride like that. I hope the man I marry will be like you."

"I hope you don't try to do what I'm doing. I'm not sure this family can handle more than one rushed wedding."

"Don't worry. I haven't met Mr. Right yet. Which reminds me. You never told me the story of how you and Katie met."

"Hmm." He rested his chin in the palm of his hand. "I'm not sure I remember."

Hailey widened her eyes. "How can you not remember something like that?"

"I don't know. We met through mutual friends. There's not much to tell." His nineteen-year-old sister was the biggest romantic he knew. If she had any idea what was really going on, she'd disown him. Good thing she was too naïve to realize what he was up to.

"Mom is beside herself that she doesn't know her future daughter-in-law. In fact, everyone is talking about how you've kept her hidden and never talked about her."

He frowned. "You know I'm a private person."

"That's what I tell people. She's adorable, and I'd think you'd want to show off the woman you love. Unless." Her eyes widened. "Is there something wrong with her? I know she looks normal, but…"

"What? No. She's a sweet girl."

"Girl?"

"Sorry. Woman."

"How old is she?"

"Twenty-three."

"Robbing the cradle?"

"She's only four years younger than me. Not a big deal at all. Now enough with the questions, Grace."

She stuck her tongue out at him. "You know I hate that nickname."

"Exactly why I used it. No more questions." He held in a chuckle. When his sister was a kid, she had the grace of an out-of-control train and had the scars to prove it. One day Renee had said she needed to take ballet to learn how to move gracefully, and the name Grace stuck.

"Fine. I won't ask about her anymore, but do you at least have a picture of her? I want to have one framed, sitting by the guest book. Actually if you have one of the two of you together that would be even better."

Having anticipated this request, he'd secretly taken a

few shots of Katie on Friday when they were shopping. He pulled up his favorite.

His sister laughed. "You're so mean. If you went around showing a picture of me biting into a muffin, you'd have to start sleeping with one eye open."

He chuckled. "You're always so dramatic. I think it's a cute picture."

Hailey giggled. "True love. Don't you have one of the two of you together?"

He slid his finger across the screen of his phone to show a selfie they'd taken at the coffee shop.

"I guess that'll do." She seemed disappointed. "I hope you'll at least have a photographer at your wedding."

"Of course. Kari White said she'd do it for us."

Hailey grinned. "Cool. When I grow up, I want to be Kari."

He chuckled. His little sis had always admired his long-time friend. They'd grown up together since they were in diapers. Many thought they'd marry one day, but marrying Kari would be like marrying his sister—gross. "If we're done here, let's go. I'll pick you up first thing tomorrow to help get everything set up. Are you sure your friends don't mind helping?"

"They're cool. I promised them each Starbucks gift cards. Don't forget!"

He pulled out his wallet and counted out one hundred dollars. "Will you take care of them for me?"

"Yes. Mom has the cake and the punch covered."

"Good." A part of him felt guilty for not being

completely honest with his family about the circumstances of this wedding. Truth was, he was afraid of how they'd make Katie feel. They wouldn't be mean—at least Hailey wouldn't—but he wanted his mom and sister to accept her as his wife and not look at her as an outsider.

Hailey stood and walked to the door leading down to the main level of The Ring. "Be honest with me, Ray. Is Katie pregnant?"

His face heated. "No."

"Okay. Mom thought maybe…"

He sighed. "I should've expected that."

Hailey punched his shoulder. "It's your own fault for not telling us about her."

"I know. But go easy on Katie. She's kind of shy. It took her a long time to warm up to me." His sister didn't need to know Katie had only started opening up to him a little over a week ago.

"Oh. I see. You were protecting her. Don't worry. I'll warn Mom. It'll be okay."

"Thanks."

Katie rubbed the rag back and forth over the craft table at the community center until her hand cramped. According to her former caseworker, Cassandra, Katie's mom was back and wanted to reconnect. Why now, after all these years was her mother interested in a relationship? She wanted to slam the door on the woman who'd rejected her, but curiosity ate at her.

"Can I go play on the basketball court?" Emily asked.

"I can't see you in there, and I need to work in this room. I'm sorry, but you'll need to stay in here with me until your ballet class starts."

Emily's bottom lip protruded. "I'm bored."

Katie sighed. What was she supposed to do with a four-year-old? Maybe keeping this job had been a mistake, but it gave her purpose, and she loved the families that frequented the center. She couldn't give up her time here.

She'd been in a rush on Thursday and hadn't done her normal thorough cleaning since she had moved that night. Then Friday, she was too worn out from lifting those heavy boxes. Now was her only time to sanitize and make sure she had everything ready to go for the art class she'd lead in another hour. "How would you like to watch a video?"

Emily's face brightened. "Yes."

Thankfully, there was a television set with an attached DVD player in this room. This would be one of the few times she'd use the TV to entertain Emily. The center also had a nice selection of G-rated videos. Katie pulled open the drawer holding all the DVDs. "Go ahead and pick out what you want to watch. Then slide it into this slot."

Emily nodded, and Katie readied the TV so Emily could do the rest on her own. With her soon-to-be niece entertained, time flew, and before she knew it, people began to trickle into the community center. "Emily, your ballet class is starting soon. We need to get you into your leotard and tights. Grab your backpack."

Emily scrambled to obey. "Hurry, Katie. I don't like being late."

Katie chuckled. She'd heard Renee say the same thing many times—like mother, like daughter. Was Katie anything like her mom? It'd been over a decade since she'd last seen her.

Emily tugged on her hand. "Come on."

"Okay. I'm coming."

They dashed to the restroom, and ten minutes later, Emily rested a hand on the wooden bar along the mirror. Slow classical music played from an ancient record player, and Emily's face scrunched in concentration. She looked to be completely engrossed in the class, so Katie returned to the craft room.

"Good afternoon." She looked from one face to another in her class of eight art students.

"Good afternoon, Miss Katie," they said in unison.

She explained what they would be drawing and showed an example from her own sketchbook. "If you have questions or need help, I'm here for you." She walked around the room and offered suggestions here and there.

Ray walked by the window that looked into the craft room and waved as he passed. She waved back. He must be going to watch Emily's ballet class. She couldn't help but smile. Ray was going to make a great dad for his niece.

"Who was that man," one of her female students

asked.

"He's…my fiancé." It felt weird saying that out loud, especially since she'd never even had a boyfriend. Her foster mom had discouraged boyfriend/girlfriend relationships when she was in high school and had instead urged her to develop strong friendships. Well, she'd had one strong friendship. There were a few guys that she liked, but she'd been too shy to do anything about it.

"You're getting married?" a boy asked.

"Yes. This Thursday."

"Wow," Breeze, another one of her female students, said. "I wish I could go. I love weddings."

"You do?" Katie had only been to one wedding as a child and had found it boring, but Breeze was one of the older kids in the group. If memory served, she was eleven and in the sixth grade. "You can come if you want."

"Really?" Her eyes widened.

"Sure. I don't have any invitations on me." She wasn't sure if they'd even printed any. "But I'll make one for you."

"Thanks!" Breeze's pace picked up on her drawing, and what had started off looking dark, rapidly changed into a bright and cheerful piece.

After thinking about how best to make an invitation, Katie tore a page from her sketchbook and cut it into fourths, then drew up several wedding invitations in case anyone else wanted to come.

She drew a rose bud in the bottom right corner, put

the information along the left side, then colored the rose red.

"What's this?"

She jumped and looked up at Ray. "I didn't realize you were standing there."

Her class giggled.

He sat beside her. "You were quite intent on that rose." He pulled one off the table and studied it. "We should make copies of this and hand them out."

"I didn't even think of making copies."

He chuckled. "If you're finished with this one, I'll run it across the street and have it printed on high quality glossy card stock. What do you think?"

"It's not necessary. I only needed one. The others were for just in case."

He shrugged. "It'll only take a few minutes. They have several self-service machines."

"Okay." She caught Breeze's eye.

The girl raised her brow and gave her a thumbs-up.

Katie laughed. "Oh, stop."

"What? He's cute."

Katie whipped her gaze toward the door to make sure Ray was out of earshot. Thankfully, he was long gone. A smile touched her lips. Her future husband was very handsome.

"I bet your mom thinks he's cute, too," Breeze said. "My mom and I talk about boys all the time."

Katie's stomach knotted at the reminder of her mom. What was she going to do? Cassandra was waiting on her decision. Thankfully, her former social worker wouldn't give her mother any information without Katie's consent. She'd always wanted to understand why her mom had left her with her dad but wasn't sure she wanted her back in her life. Even after years of counseling, a part of her was still angry with the woman that was supposed to nurture and protect her. What if Mom was as big of a mess as Dad?

9

Monday evening Ray glanced at Katie sitting at the far end of the couch. She looked good in his living room. "I'm relieved Emily's sleeping better. Bringing the contents of her bedroom here was genius. I wish I'd thought of it."

"I'm glad she's not so upset. Her grief counselor is probably helping as well."

"Maybe." He wasn't sure how much good the woman was doing. He hadn't seen any improvement until Katie started taking care of her. Now Emily was more content. Not herself yet, but perhaps her new self. "Did you pass out the invitations I had printed?"

"A few. Some of the kids in my art class want to come." She shrugged. "We'll see if they do or not."

"Either way, it was nice that they wanted to."

She nodded and folded her hands in her lap. "Do you think you could help me with something? Normally I'd ask Brandi, but with her wedding this weekend, I hate to bother her."

"I'll do my best." He shifted to better face her and wished they were closer. The thought surprised him. Then again, over the past week, they'd spent a lot of time together and had grown closer than he'd expected in such a short period.

"I received a call from my social worker earlier today."

"You have a social worker?" Now this was news.

"No. Not now. She handled my case when I was in foster care."

"Oh, I see. Why would she be calling you so many years later?"

"She checks up on me from time to time. But that's not why she called." Katie took a deep breath and let it out slowly as if to calm herself. "My mom is back and wants to connect with me. I don't know what to do."

"Whoa. That's big." Now he understood why she was jumpy after taking that call.

She shrugged. "I've thought about it all day, and I'm no closer to a solution. I think about Emily and how she'd do anything to see her mom again. I feel ungrateful because I'm not sure I want to see mine." She looked his way, and their gazes locked.

Hurt, pain, and confusion filled her eyes. "Does that make me a bad person?"

"No. It makes you human."

"Thanks."

"Maybe you should make a list of pros and cons."

"You sound like Renee."

He chuckled. "I do, don't I?" He was glad they

could share memories of his sister and that Katie wasn't afraid to talk about her. He reached across the cushion between them and grasped her hand. "Pros?"

"I'd like to see if we look anything alike. She took off so long ago my memory has faded since the one picture I had as a kid was taken away." She looked to him. "One of my foster parents confiscated it as a punishment and never gave it back."

"That was a bit excessive and mean." He fisted his free hand. It was no wonder she was cautious around people she didn't know well. He hurt for her and wished he could give her a do-over.

"Perhaps, but I probably deserved it. I was a very troubled girl and acted out a lot."

"I can't imagine." He really couldn't. From what he'd seen, Katie was a sweet, mild-mannered woman with a kind heart. This person she hinted at did not sound like her at all. "But back to the list. You want to see what she looks like. It's probably good to get a medical history, too, if she's willing."

"Good point. But I don't know if I want a relationship with her."

"Maybe she's changed."

"It's possible. I sure have." She ducked her head.

He smiled. "Why are you suddenly the color of a perfectly cooked lobster?"

"I still can't believe I proposed to you."

He chuckled. "You were braver than me. I was going to, but I got cold feet."

She sat up straight and turned her body to face him.

"Seriously. You planned to propose? When?"

"That day I requested you come to my office, but then I felt like I'd be putting you on the spot and didn't ask, even though I felt the Lord tell me to ask you."

"Do you mean to tell me you were really going to ask me?" She grinned and the bright red faded to her normal color.

He nodded. "After you planted the idea in my mind that night at the diner, I couldn't let it go."

She giggled.

He chuckled. "What?"

"Oh, nothing. I just find this very amusing—to think I felt self-conscious about being the one to propose. I don't feel that way anymore."

"Good." He pulled her closer and hugged her to his side. "I have high hopes for us, Katie. And I enjoy spending time with you like this."

She stilled in his arm. "Yeah. Me, too," she said softly. She shifted and her eyes met his.

His breath hitched. If he didn't know better he'd think he read love there. Clearly, he wasn't good at reading women, because there was no way she had strong feelings for him—yet. Then again, his own were rapidly moving in that direction. He drew closer to her.

She blinked and broke the contact. "I still don't know what to do about my mom."

He dragged his mind back to the topic. "I suggest you continue to think through the pros and cons. Then pray and consider the worst that could happen if you do let her into your life."

"Good advice. I suppose we could meet on neutral ground, set up by Cassandra, then go from there. I don't have to let her into my life to meet with her."

"True. And if you need backup, I could come along."

Her eyes widened. "You'd do that for me?"

"Absolutely." He placed a kiss on the top of her head. "It's getting late."

She sat up then stood. "You're right, and Emily doesn't sleep in either. 'Night, Ray."

"I'll walk you to your door. I don't like the idea of you being outside alone at this time of night, even if it is a short distance." They lived in a relatively safe neighborhood, but he was suddenly feeling protective.

"Thanks." A smile lit her eyes. "It's only ten, but I won't turn down the escort." She slipped her hand around his arm and walked silently beside him all the way to her apartment door. She turned to him. "Good night."

He touched a hand to her face—so soft. Somehow, she already held his heart.

Her eyes widened, and she stilled.

"May I kiss you?" he spoke the words softly.

She nodded in the glow of the garage light.

His lips met hers ever so briefly—a teaser for what was to come—some day, he hoped. "Sleep well." He waited until he heard the lock slip into place then went back inside his house. Though he couldn't honestly say he loved her, could it be too much to hope for good things to come for them?

Katie touched a finger to her lips as she stood on the

other side of her apartment door. She'd never sleep now! There was no way her mind would shut off after such a sweet kiss. She yawned…then again, maybe she could sleep. She had a four-year-old to care for all day tomorrow.

How was it she could feel so many different emotions in one evening? Fear, frustration, confusion, contentment, peace, and dare she go there—love. No, it was too soon. What they shared wasn't love. It couldn't be. Strong liking was more accurate. Yes, she very much liked Ray and hoped that things would continue to progress with him, but there was so much more to consider. Her mom for starters. She needed to get back to Cassandra as soon as possible if she was going to meet her mom. She wanted to do it before the wedding, which left tomorrow or Wednesday. *What do I do, Lord?*

She quickly readied for bed then clicked off the lamp. Maybe she'd know what to do by morning.

A buzzing sound awakened Katie. She opened her eyes and squinted at the sun shining in from the windows. She reached over and grabbed her phone. "Hello."

"I'm sorry to wake you."

"Cassandra?"

"Yes. Your mom is sitting beside my desk."

Katie sat straight up. "What is she doing there? Can she hear us talking?"

"No. I walked out of earshot, but I can still see her."

"What does she want?"

"She says she only wants to see you."

"What should I do? How does she look?"

"She looks put together. Whether you meet her or not is your choice."

Katie fisted her hand around the sheets. "I don't know. I want to see her, but I don't want to open the door to a relationship with her."

"Why not meet at a neutral place like a Starbucks. You'd at least be able to see what she looks like now and then make a decision at that point."

"How will I know who she is?" Katie would never recognize her mom after all these years. She could barely remember what she used to look like.

"Trust me. You'll know."

"Okay. I'll do it." She had questions she wanted answered, and this might be her only chance to find out the answers.

"I'll tell her to be there in an hour," Cassandra said.

"Whoa. It's not that simple. I need time to plan. I'm a nanny, and I can't bring a four-year-old along."

"Why not?"

"Never mind. I'll figure something out." She rambled off the address of the Starbucks around the corner from The Ring. "Go ahead and tell her I'll meet her there, but make it two hours."

"Okay. Let me know how it goes."

"Sure. I don't suppose you want to join us?"

"I can't. Swamped as usual."

"Okay. I know you said I'd know her, but will you tell me what she looks like anyway?

"She has red hair, and she's wearing a Mariners' T-shirt."

"Thanks." Decision made, she quickly readied herself then raced down the stairs and into Ray's house. "Morning." She went straight for the coffeepot.

"What are you doing?" Ray asked.

"I'm meeting my mom in two hours at Starbucks."

He took the pot from her hand. "Go easy on that stuff. I make it super strong. You'll get the shakes if you drink a whole cup."

"Oh, thanks for the warning. I'm already shaking." Her gaze shot around the kitchen. "Where's Emily? She's usually up by now."

"Hailey stopped by a few minutes ago and took her."

"Was that planned?" She frowned. As Emily's nanny, she ought to have a handle on the girl's schedule.

"Hailey called early this morning. She'll drop Emily at the community center this afternoon." He looked her way. "I know you think Emily shouldn't spend a lot of time with my sister, but Hailey is hurting, too, and being with Emily is good for her."

"You're right. I didn't think of that." She hadn't wanted to bring Emily, but over the past thirty minutes she'd decided having Emily along might be a nice buffer. Then again, Katie had no idea what kind of person her mom was. It was probably best not to have Emily come along.

"Hey." Ray faced her and rested his hands on her shoulders. "Are you okay? I can come with you if you need moral support."

Did she want him there? Yes. But shouldn't she do this on her own? "I don't know. What if she's horrible?"

"What if she's wonderful? I'd like to meet her."

"Why? And I guarantee she's not wonderful. She abandoned me with an abusive father." She slapped a hand to her mouth. She had not meant to reveal that. No one knew. She'd kept that hidden from everyone.

Ray frowned. "Your dad hurt you?"

She nodded. Years of keeping her secret hidden and suddenly revealing it burst a dam. Her throat thickened. She looked away. "I need to go."

"Why?" He removed his hands from her shoulders.

Cold filled the area where his hands had been. She had to look pathetic in his eyes; breaking down in front of him was not an option.

"Let me be here for you, Katie." His voice softened. "That's what good friends do."

Her watery eyes met his. A tear escaped. She turned her face, refusing to give in to the overwhelming emotions attacking her. She took a shuttering breath.

"Ah, Katie. Come here." He gently drew her to him and held her.

Her face heated as tears burned her throat. Ray's heartbeat pulsed in her ear. Overcome with his tender care, a sob ripped through her.

Ray's arms tightened around her.

How could her mom have left her with Dad? She'd known what he was like. She should have taken Katie with her. Tears flowed unchecked. Her body shook, and she clung to Ray.

109

His hand gently rubbed her back. He didn't offer any words, only silent support.

The wracking tears finally stopped. She took a deep breath and let it out. "I'm sorry. I'm okay now." She lowered her hands to her side and stepped out of his embrace.

He tore a paper towel off the roll and handed it to her.

"Thanks. I didn't mean to lose it on you."

"You have nothing to be sorry for. How do you feel now?"

She splashed water on her face then dried it with the towel. "Embarrassed but relieved at the same time. It feels good to finally tell someone."

"What can I do?"

"Nothing. I'm fine."

"I'm not. I'm boiling mad that you were hurt like that."

Her eyes widened. His anger was nothing compared to her dad's rage. He was a violent drunk, and one night he hit the wrong person—a cop—and when the man fell, he struck his head and died. "When my dad went to prison, it was a relief. But at the same time, I was only thirteen, and I was scared, and angry, too. My parents failed me, and it hurt."

"What did your dad do to you?"

"He hit me when he got drunk. But he was smart. He only hit me where he knew no one would see."

"Did he hurt your mom, too?"

Katie nodded. She'd never abandon her own child

like her mother had.

"I'd like to come with you today." His voice was soft yet firm.

"Okay. But let me do the talking."

"Fine, but I won't let her hurt you anymore." His fierce gaze bore into hers. "I'm serious. One misstep on her part and we're leaving."

She nodded and swallowed the sudden lump in her throat. "Thanks. I need to go redo my face."

"I'll make us breakfast."

She rushed up to her apartment in a daze-like state. Without a doubt, Ray was a good man—the kind of man who seemed to only exist in her dreams. That wasn't fair though. Ian was also a good guy. She was so thankful neither of them drank. There was no way she'd ever get involved with a guy who drank, even if he didn't get drunk—too many bad memories to go there. She washed her face and reapplied a light coat of makeup. Her normal jeans and T-shirt suddenly didn't feel right. She grabbed the black A-line skirt she reserved for special occasions and her favorite red top then slipped into black ballet flats. If she was going to see her mom today, she wanted to look her best.

Ray glanced over his shoulder when she entered the kitchen. "You changed."

"Too much?" She looked down at the ensemble.

"Just right. And you won't need your coat to hide in either." He flipped two pancakes onto a plate.

She stuck her tongue out at him.

He chuckled. "Syrup's in the fridge."

"Thanks. They're gluten free?" There was no way

she could eat. Her stomach was a mess with nerves, but she'd try for Ray.

"Of course. I used the mix you bought. He grabbed his plate and parked himself beside her. "Eat up. I know I'm not the best cook, but I make decent pancakes."

She forked a bite into her mouth and chewed.

He chuckled. "I take it back. These are terrible. Let's go out."

"These are fine."

He took her plate and placed it in the sink. "If the look on your face when you were chewing is any indication, they are far from fine."

She grimaced. "I'm sorry. I think anything I eat this morning will taste like wood. I'm supposed to meet my mom at Starbucks. You want to grab something there?"

"Sounds good. Be right back." A few minutes later, he returned.

She couldn't believe she was marrying this man— and in only two days! Would they have the kind of marriage she'd witnessed in Brandi's parents? She hoped so. Even though she ended up with a wonderful foster family, she hadn't been especially close to them. Brandi's parents welcomed her into their home and had been the mentors she'd needed. Too bad they wouldn't be able to attend her wedding. They were probably the only other people she would have chosen to invite.

Ray rested a hand on her shoulder. "You okay?"

"Yes. I was lost in thought, but I'm fine." She plastered on a smile. "Let's get this over with." She only hoped she wasn't making a huge mistake.

10

Katie recognized her mother the moment the woman walked into Starbucks. "There she is," she whispered to Ray.

"You could be twins, except for the hair color."

She nodded—her mouth too dry to speak. She sipped her water then stood. Her mother's gaze landed on her, and she stopped mid-step.

"Katie?" Her face broke into a smile. She rushed forward. "Thank you for meeting me." She opened her arms.

Katie sidestepped the embrace. "Mom, this is my fiancé, Ray."

Ray nodded.

"You're engaged? I didn't expect that." She frowned.

"Why's that?" Katie asked, trying to keep a neutral tone but failing miserably as years of pent up anger suddenly overcame her.

Mom's smile faded. "You're too young. I don't want

you to make the same mistake I did." She stood. "Excuse me. I'm going to grab something to drink. Be right back. You won't leave, will you?"

"I'll wait." Katie sat, keeping her gaze on her mother. Dizziness hit her as she tried to calm the rage that coursed through her. What right did her mother have to criticize her or offer advice? She gave up that right when she walked away.

Ray grasped her hand and gave it a light squeeze. "What can I do for you?"

"Pray. I didn't realize how angry I was until I saw her. I don't want to make a scene or embarrass you." Her gaze met his. "I'm sorry for what she said."

"Don't be. She's right. You're young, but you're also mature."

"But, still, she has no right to judge me."

He ducked his head and got in her face. "Remember you're a child of the King. He loves you more than we can imagine. He's here for you, Katie."

She nodded as her mother carried a pink colored Frappuccino back to their table. Ray was right. She was God's child first and foremost. Her mom was human and imperfect. Everyone messed up—some more than others.

Mom sat across from them. "Thank you for meeting me. I know it wasn't easy. I didn't think you'd agree considering our history. But I had to try." Her mom's demeanor had changed to business.

"You're right. It wasn't easy. Why did you want to meet?" She had so many questions.

"I needed to apologize. I'm sorry for not taking you with me or sticking around."

"Why did you leave?"

"I had a nervous breakdown. Ended up in the psych ward, and once I was released, I couldn't go back. It was too much. I was so afraid."

"So you left your ten-year-old daughter to deal with Dad instead? Why didn't you at least turn him in?"

"I was afraid. He knew where I was and—"

"Wait. Dad knew you were in the hospital?" He'd told her that Mom had run away because she didn't want to be a mom anymore. She should have known he was lying.

"Yes. He was listed as my emergency contact. When they released me, I told him I wanted a divorce and that I wanted you, but he threatened me. I was too weak to fight him. So I moved away and started a new life. I recently learned your dad was in prison. Or I would have come sooner."

"You're thirteen years too late." She didn't buy for one minute that no one ever tried to contact her mother when her dad was arrested.

Mom frowned. "I know. I have regrets. You're my biggest. I'm so sorry. Please forgive me. I hope it's not too late for us."

"I'll try, but it's safe to say there will never be anything between us."

Ray cleared his throat.

She'd almost forgotten he was there. She shot a look in his direction and raised a brow.

"Perhaps you both need time to get used to the idea of each other," Ray said. "Expecting to pick up where you left off is unrealistic."

He had a point. Maybe given time…no, all the time in the world would change nothing. That would take a miracle.

"What if the two of you agree to meet here once a week for the next month and see what happens?"

Katie shot him a look she hoped would silence him. She appreciated that he was here for her but didn't care for him butting in. She looked to her mother to gauge her reaction.

"A month is impossible."

Whew!

"But I suppose I could stick around for another week or two."

So much for that. She'd look like the bad guy if she turned down her mother's offer. "What do you do for a living?"

"I cut hair."

"Then how can you afford to be away for so long?"

She grinned. "I'm very expensive."

"Okay. Fine. I'll meet you here every Monday evening for the next two weeks."

"Evening?"

"I have a job."

"Of course."

They firmed up their plans.

"What if one of us needs to cancel?" Her mom asked. "How will I contact you?"

"Tell Cassandra. She'll make sure I get the message. Make sure she has your number, too."

"Okay. Thanks." Her mother's gaze encompassed both Katie and Ray before she stood and walked out.

Katie blew out a breath and sagged in her chair. "I wish you hadn't done that."

"I realized that once it was too late. How are you doing?"

"I was better before she came back into my life." At least she didn't ask to come to their wedding!

Thursday morning, Katie awoke to sunshine streaming through the apartment windows. She'd be a married woman by day's end. There'd been no wedding rehearsal last night, but she and Ray would be meeting with his minister today, who, according to Ray, understood the circumstances of their marriage, which was the only reason he'd agreed to officiate without pre-marital counseling. She kicked the covers off her twin bed, grabbed the jeans she'd picked out last night and a pastel pink t-shirt, then padded to the bathroom.

It would be a long day since she still had to work her shift at the community center this afternoon. But she could handle it all.

A knock on her door startled her. She walked over to it and pulled it open.

"Happy birthday!" Brandi held a bouquet of balloons and a pastry box. "Aren't you going to invite me in?"

"Yes. Sorry. You took me by surprise. I completely forgot about my birthday. I can't believe I'm getting married this young. Somehow I thought I'd fall in love and get married closer to thirty." If anyone had told her she'd be getting married on her twenty-fourth birthday she'd have laughed. But as it was, no one but Brandi even knew. She took extra care with her hair.

"I know how you are about birthdays," Brandi said. "I wondered if you'd remember this year with all that's been going on."

Katie had gotten into the habit of forgetting about her special day when she was younger to avoid being disappointed—birthdays had always been a letdown when she was a kid. She stepped aside. "What are you doing here? Why aren't you at work?"

"My last day was yesterday. I'm here to help however you need me." Brandi strode past Katie and set the balloons and box on the kitchen counter. "You couldn't have timed this wedding better, well except my parents won't be back in time for it."

"It's okay. At least I get to have you there. I'm surprised you're so enthusiastic. I thought you didn't approve."

"I might not think what you're doing is the best for you, but that doesn't change that you're my friend, and I want to support you and be there to help you."

Katie hugged her. "Thank you. This means a lot."

Brandi looked around the apartment. "So what are we doing today?"

"Ray and I meet with the minister at ten. Then we

were going to grab lunch. I wish I'd known what you were planning."

"Not a problem. Do you have the marriage license?"

"Yes. We applied for that before we moved the date up. Ray has it."

"Good. What about your dress? I can make sure it gets to The Ring safely, and I can prepare snacks so you don't faint from low blood sugar."

"Very funny. You know I don't faint, and my dress is already at The Ring. There's little to do since Ray's taking care of everything."

Disappointment washed over Brandi's face. "So there's nothing I can do for you today?"

"You could hang out with me and keep me sane. I have to work this afternoon, and it'd be fun to have you along. Thankfully, Hailey is taking Emily again today, so that will make things a lot easier."

"I agree, but why are you working on your wedding day? No one does that."

"I do." She didn't want to make a big deal about getting married to anyone at work other than those who already knew. If she'd taken the afternoon off, there'd have been so many questions. Questions she didn't want to answer.

"Don't I need to have a background check or something to volunteer?"

"Normally, yes, but you won't be alone. It's a one-time thing. Say yes. It will be so much more fun."

"Sure. Why not? You're my agenda today."

"Thanks! So what's in the bag?"

"A gluten free scone for you, and in this bag is a glazed donut for me. I know it's not a healthy start to the day, but it'll be a sweet one." She giggled. "You like how I did that? *Sweet* one."

"And I thought I was the geek." Katie took a bite of a scone and wished for something to wash it down with. "You want a glass of milk?"

"Sure."

They finished their treat then headed downstairs at the same time that Ray was backing out of the garage. He stopped and put down the window.

"Good morning! I'll be back in time to get you for our appointment."

"Brandi can take me. We'll meet you there."

"We? Brandi is coming too?"

Katie grinned and nodded her head. The surprise on Ray's face was priceless. "See you later," she tossed over her shoulder as she strutted to Brandi's car. Once inside, they busted up laughing "What is it about birthdays that makes me act like an adolescent? And don't you dare tell him it's my birthday. I don't want him to know."

Brandi chuckled. "I can't believe he didn't figure it out when you were filling out the application for a marriage license. I'm sure he'll figure it out. After all, before the day is over, you'll be married." Brandi waved her hand over Katie. "Girl, do you realize you just flirted with your future husband? I don't think I've ever seen you flirt with anyone! What gives?"

"Nothing. I was unaware I was flirting." But she didn't mind in the least that she had been. She gasped.

She really and truly loved Ray—when had that happened? Sure, she'd had a crush on him, but that was a lot different than love. Who was she trying to kid? It was now clear she'd loved Ray practically from the day she'd met him. If only he loved her back. She needed Ray to fall in love with her because she wasn't sure she'd last six months being in love alone. It would hurt too much.

"There you are."

Ray whirled around. "Mom, this is the men's locker room."

She raised a brow. "Do I look like I care?" She straightened his black bow tie. "You've been avoiding me."

"Not true. I've been swamped."

"You never mentioned Katie before your sister died. Why the sudden rush to marry?"

He told her about Brandi and Ian leaving the country.

"You've known about that for how long?" She raised a brow.

He shrugged. There was no way he was getting out of this conversation unscathed. "You'll like Katie once you get to know her. She's very sweet, and you have something in common."

"Something I could have found out on my own if you'd had the courtesy to introduce us at a decent time rather than when—" Her voice caught. "I refuse to cry. But you know what I was going to say."

"Yes, and I'm sorry you met that way."

She rested a hand on his arm. "Do you love her, Ray?"

He looked away. "She's very special. I care about her a lot."

"You didn't answer me."

"I need to get out there."

"Trust me. The wedding won't happen without you. Now what is going on? This isn't like you."

He sighed. "It's complicated."

"Clearly." Mom crossed her arms. "I hope you know what you're doing." She turned and marched from the locker room.

Ian approached. A worried look settled on his face. "Sorry, I couldn't help overhearing. Are you okay?"

"Yeah." How was Katie doing? She had been in good spirits the last time he'd seen her today. In spite of his mother's ire, marrying Katie when she could have her best friend with her was the right decision.

"Okay. You ready?"

Ray nodded. "Ready as I'll ever be." They stepped out of the locker room into the gym. Two rows of folding chairs were set up facing the boxing ring. As promised, Rusty had the ropes removed from one side and added centered stairs. The ring had been transformed into a stage.

Hailey and her friends had done the impossible. They'd turned this gym into something beautiful. A white arbor with vines woven through it stood in the center of the ring. A white runner went down the center between the rows of chairs and up the stairs all the way to the arbor. A violinist and a cellist sat off to the side playing classical music.

He walked up the stairs to where the minister waited.

"You ready for this?"

Ray nodded. "I think so. Have you seen Katie?"

"Yes, and your bride looks lovely. Here she comes."

Katie walked up the stairs. His eyes took her in from head to toe. The overhead lights caught on his bride's sparkly headpiece. He sucked in a breath. The white dress was perfect. She held a simple bouquet of red roses. He let his eyes roam further and noted her fancy white sneakers. He held in a chuckle, afraid she'd bolt if he laughed.

Katie stopped beside him. Her lipstick stood out on her pale face. Had she suddenly become sick?

He slipped his hand around her ice-cold hand and gave it a gentle squeeze. "You okay?" he whispered.

"Yes." A wobbly smile tipped her lips.

The minister spoke briefly then prompted them in saying their vows.

Ray pulled Katie's ring from his pocket. He'd finally found the perfect ring and kept it a surprise. She widened her eyes when he took her hand and slipped the simple filigree band in white gold onto her finger. After searching for an engagement ring together, she'd decided she didn't want one, and told people as much when they asked. Apparently she didn't like wearing jewelry. He hoped this simple, yet elegant, ring would please her, but it was difficult to tell.

The minister handed Katie his ring, and she slipped it onto his finger. It fit like it was made for him. Vintage or not, it was perfect.

"I now pronounce you husband and wife. You may kiss your bride."

Ray looked down at his wife and saw fear in her eyes. He wrapped one arm around her shoulder the other around her waist, drew her close, and whispered in her ear, "Are you okay? We don't have to kiss."

She titled her head and kissed him ever so softly.

His insides jolted. He kissed her back for only a moment before she stepped away.

"I present to you Mr. and Mrs. O'Brien."

Their guests clapped.

"Please join Ray and Katie at the community center down the street for their reception."

Ray looked around the room and realized for the first time that he knew everyone in the room. "Where are the guests you invited?" he asked close to her ear.

"Brandi's in the front row." She smiled and blinked shiny eyes.

He assisted her down the stairs. They paused for pictures and congratulations from his friends.

His mother and sister slipped up the stairs with Emily probably to get the punch and cake ready.

He wrapped an arm around Katie's trembling shoulder. "We'll see you at the reception," he said to no one in particular.

Once outside and alone with her, he reached for her

hand. "Katie look at me."

She turned to him. "What?" Her voice came out in a whisper.

"What's wrong?"

"Nothing."

"I may not know you as well as a husband ought to know his wife, but I know you well enough to know when something is wrong. What happened?"

She shook her head and faced forward. "It doesn't matter. Let's go cut the cake and get this over with."

Her words felt like a sucker punch. He'd thought they were on the way to something special, but clearly he'd read the situation wrong. What had happened?

11

Katie couldn't stop the trembling even as she attempted to pull off the greatest acting of her life while smiling and feeding a piece of cake to Ray—her husband—a man who, according to his mother, was too good for her. Clapping yanked her from her thoughts.

Ray kept a hand lightly on her back. "How long do we have to stick around for this?" He leaned close and spoke through the side of his mouth.

It sounded like he was as ready as she to escape the facade of a happily married couple. What had she been thinking?

Hailey walked up to Katie and hugged her. "Welcome to the family."

Ray grinned. "Thanks for all your help, sis. We never would have pulled this off without you."

Katie slipped a hand around Ray's arm. "Your brother is in a hurry to get out of here. Is there any way we can leave sooner than later?"

Hailey shot her brother a knowing look. "I don't see

why not. I'll make sure the gifts and cards get to the house, and my friends will help with clean up." She rested a hand on Katie's shoulder. "Before you go, be sure to toss the bouquet. I understand wanting to get out of here. This is the dullest wedding reception I've ever attended." She smacked a hand over her mouth.

Ray chuckled. "It's okay. I'm not offended since you're the one who planned it."

Hailey's face blossomed pink. "Guilty. I'm so sorry, but the wedding was my thing. I delegated the reception to mom."

That explained the lack of decorations and plain sheet cake that wasn't gluten free so Katie couldn't even taste it. She should never have expected a wedding cake, but somehow she'd thought…it didn't matter.

"Excuse me." Hailey waved a hand at the guests. "Ray and Katie are anxious to get their honeymoon started, so Katie is going to toss her bouquet, and then they'll be off. All single ladies please line up over here."

Ten minutes later, they'd said their good-byes and were on their way out when Ray's mother stopped them.

"When you return home, I expect you to properly introduce me to your bride. You will come for Sunday lunch."

Emily let go of her grandmother's leg and wrapped her arms around Ray's leg. "I love you, Uncle Ray. When will you get me from Grandma's?"

He picked her up. "I'll tell you what. Your Aunt Katie and I aren't going on a honeymoon yet. How about you come home with us now?"

That had been the plan all along, and his mother knew it, so this conversation made no sense. What was she up to now?

Ray's mother frowned, clearly disapproving of their plans. "It's not fitting to have a child in the house on your honeymoon night. Miss Emily will be staying with me tonight. You may pick her up in the morning if you would like."

Ray shot his mom a look of surprise then focused his attention on his niece. "What do you think, squirt?"

Emily nodded and planted a kiss on his cheek. "See you tomorrow. 'Bye, Aunt Katie."

"Good-bye." Even though they'd been talking about it all week, it felt odd to have Emily call her *Aunt*— another adjustment for them both, but her niece seemed to have no trouble with the change, so she'd try to adjust quickly.

Ray set Emily down then guided Katie out the door to his waiting car, which no one had thought to decorate. It was just as well. Ray opened the passenger door and waited for her to be situated before closing it. He slid in the driver's side, and a moment later, they were off.

Katie had so many questions, but talking took too much energy. She couldn't wait to get back to her apartment. Or would he expect her to move to the house tonight? They hadn't talked about when she would move in. She'd finished painting, so there was nothing stopping her.

"You're quiet."

"I'm tired." It was true. Today had been one of the

longest days of her life. She was sure the moment her head hit the pillow she would have slept, were it not for her mother-in-law's hurtful words shortly before the wedding. That woman had it in her head that Katie had seduced her son—as if!

"About my mom."

"Can we talk tomorrow, Ray? All I want to do right now is bury my head in my pillow." Plus, talking about that horrible woman on her wedding day would ruin any good memories she might have had.

"Okay. I arranged for you to have the rest of the week off at the community center. Had I known you were scheduled to work today, I'd have arranged today off for you as well."

"Why?" She whipped her attention in his direction. "You had no right. I depend on that income." They were barely married, and he was trying to run her life—it wasn't even a real marriage! Well, that would stop right now.

"Whoa." His hands tightened on the steering wheel. "Most people think we're on our honeymoon. It will look a little strange if either of us show up at work tomorrow."

"Oh, I see your point. But you told your mom we're taking our honeymoon later."

"Only because of Emily. Otherwise, I'd have let her believe we were honeymooning now, too."

Katie blinked away tears of frustration. Why had she been so emotional lately?

"I thought we could use that time to ourselves.

We'll have Emily along, but that'll be good. We need to bond as a family."

Her stomach clenched. "Sure, you're right." Emily needed a stable home life. After all, that was why she was here. "But I didn't expect you to alter my work schedule without my knowledge or permission."

He stopped at a red light. "Sorry. I'm new at this marriage thing. Clearly, that was a rookie mistake. But you requested that I get to know you before we married. Since the wedding happened so fast, I didn't get to hold up my end of the agreement. I'd like to fix that now."

"Oh." She clenched her hands in her lap. "What do you have in mind?"

"Tomorrow is supposed to be a nice spring day. I thought we could do something outdoors. Play tourist, rent canoes, go for a sail, hike, whatever you'd like. We have all day."

"Oh." Her heart melted. Now she wished he hadn't offered to pick up Emily in the morning. She'd love to spend a couple of days alone with Ray. "I'd like that. I'm sure Emily will as well."

He chuckled. "I think we might wait to get her until a little later in the day. I never should have said we'd bring her along. I'll call her when we get home."

The light changed, and they pulled forward.

"That's a nice idea."

Ray might be new at this being married thing, as he put it, but he was already proving to be adept. "If you don't mind though, I'll let you pick her up. Your mother hates me." She'd known from the start Ray's mom wasn't the nicest, but after tonight, she wanted to avoid her as much as possible. The uptight, mean woman who'd cornered her right before the wedding had sent her reeling.

"I'd argue, but I think you might be right. I know you can win her over in time."

Fat chance. Had she known how awful Ray's mom was before all of this, she might not have offered to marry him. It was too late now. Somehow, they all had to make it work and, hopefully, come out unscathed.

Ray pulled into his driveway and killed the engine. He didn't want to leave Katie like this. She'd hinted at a problem with his mom. He needed to know what was said. He rested a hand on Katie's arm to stop her from getting out. "Can we visit before you turn in? There's something we should talk about."

"Can it wait until morning? I really am tired."

He motioned toward the house. "Why not move into the house tonight? I'd sleep better if we were both under the same roof."

She opened her mouth, presumably to protest.

"I'll help you pack what you need. You don't have to bring everything over tonight." Maybe she would talk about what was bothering her while they packed up her stuff.

"I guess. But I don't need help. I'll grab what I need and meet you over there."

He sighed. So much for that idea.

Later that night, Ray lay in bed, his mind wandering. What had happened to cause Katie to shut down? She'd been fine earlier in the day when Brandi was with them. He'd left Katie with Brandi to get ready for the wedding and hadn't seen her again until she walked down the aisle. Something had definitely changed.

The most troubling part—that kiss. Another thing ate at him—she hadn't said what she thought of the ring he'd given her.

He'd ended up at the same pawnshop where she'd purchased his ring since she'd refused to wear anything too big or fancy. He'd found the simple filigree band in white gold—not the same quality she'd purchased for him, but the delicate design suited her. He'd been so pleased with the purchase and thought for sure she would love it, but instead he only got silence.

He punched down his pillow and shifted to his side. This day had not turned out at all like he'd expected. Unable to sleep, he kicked off the covers. As he exited his room, he noticed the light on under the closed door to Katie's room. It looked like he wasn't the only one who couldn't sleep.

Downstairs, he eased into his favorite recliner and opened the book he'd been reading. The words all blurred together, and he slammed the cover shut. This was ridiculous. Clearly, they were both too keyed up to sleep. Katie might have declared she was tired, but he suspected they both needed time to decompress after the whirlwind of the past week.

He made two mugs of hot chocolate and headed

back upstairs. He knocked softly.

"Ray?"

"Yes. May I come in?"

The door opened, and she poked her head around. Her face softened when her eyes landed on the mugs. "Come in."

She wore spandex with a snug-fitting hot pink T-shirt over it and slippers that had the face of a pig on each foot. He grinned and pointed to her feet. "Nice look."

"Thanks. What are you doing?"

He held out a mug. "I couldn't sleep and saw your light on. I made us hot chocolate—gluten free."

She looked down at the mug, and a smile tugged at her lips. "You added whipped cream."

"Of course. May I sit?" He pointed to the chair in the corner.

"Sure. As tired as I am, I can't sleep either. This mattress feels so different from mine." She placed the mug onto the nightstand then propped a pile of pillows onto the bed and pulled the covers over herself. "Your sister did a nice job with the wedding."

"Hailey's a trooper. Although without Rusty, she never could have made the boxing ring into a stage. I wish my mom would've gone to a little effort with the reception. I feel badly about that."

"You do?" Her gaze held his. Doubt filled her eyes.

His stomach knotted. "Of course." Why would Katie question his desire to have a nice reception? Their marriage might be non-traditional, but he still wanted the best for his bride. He cared about Katie. Surely, she knew that.

She dropped her focus to the mug. "I know why I can't sleep, but why can't you?"

"I suspect for the same reason."

"I doubt that." She sipped the hot chocolate. "This is good."

"Thanks. Today was quite a day. All things considered, it turned out well. Don't you think?"

She nodded, keeping her focus on her drink. She still wasn't acting like the Katie he'd come to know. "Something happened today that upset you. I'd like to help if I can."

She tilted her face but not before he saw a tear stream down her cheek.

His heart broke. "Ah, Katie. Please talk to me. Tell me what's wrong." He moved to the bed and sat on the edge beside her.

She shook her head, still not looking at him.

"I care about you. I want to be there for you. Please let me."

She sniffled and wiped her face with the back of her hand. "Thank you. But I don't think your mother would approve. In fact, I think it would upset her."

He set his mug on her nightstand. "What's that supposed to mean?"

Silence met him.

"Katie, in order for this to work, I need you to talk to me." He touched a finger to her chin and gently tipped her face so he could see it.

She set the mug aside, pulled her knees to her chest, and rested her cheek on them. "I'll be fine, Ray."

Her eyes shone, but he saw something there he hadn't noticed before—determination. "I have no doubt. You're tougher than I realized. But I want to know what happened with my mom. I know something did. She was in rare form before our wedding. And based on your comment, I'm guessing she cornered you like she did me."

"She harassed you, too?" Surprise lit her eyes.

He nodded. Anger surged through him. It was one thing for his mom to question him, but she'd crossed the line if she went after Katie. He desperately wanted to hold his wife but it was too soon. She was like a frightened kitten tonight, and he needed to tread carefully. "What did my mom say to you?"

"It's nothing you need to worry about. Believe me. I've heard worse, but it hurt coming from her. Even though we've gotten off to a rough start, I'd hoped for a good relationship with her, but after tonight, I realize your mom and I will never be friends."

Based on what he knew of Katie's past, he had no doubt, but she shouldn't have to take garbage from his mother. "How about you let me decide what to worry about?" He kept his voice gentle even though he was frustrated. "Will you please tell me what she said?"

"I can't." Her voice caught.

"I know it's difficult, but it's important. Please."

She gnawed on her bottom lip. "She said that I'm a tramp and not worthy of you."

He clamped his teeth together. He'd deal with his mother later, but right now, Katie needed him. He blew out a slow breath and nudged her over. "Mind if I share the pillows?"

She hesitated then scooted over to the middle of the bed. He leaned against the pile of fluffy pillows propped against the headboard and stretched out his legs atop the covers. "Thanks. This is much more comfortable. My mom was way out of line, and I'll make sure she understands that talking to you like that is not okay, nor will it be tolerated in the future."

Katie gasped. "Seriously? You'll stand up to her for me?"

"Absolutely." He shifted to face her and took her hand, cradling it between his. "You are my wife. Maybe we aren't starting in the same place as most couples, but as my wife, I expect you to be treated with kindness and respect by my family. Especially my mother." He ducked his head to meet her gaze. "I'll take care of this."

"Thanks."

He chuckled. "Why do you look baffled?"

"I'm not used to people sticking up for me like that."

His heart broke. "I wish that wasn't the case, but I promise from this moment forward, it won't be. I'm here for you."

She nodded and a lone tear slid down her cheek. She palmed it away. "You're a good man, Ray. I'm glad I married you. I only wish your mom felt toward me a smidgen of what I feel for you."

He gave her hand a squeeze before lacing his fingers through it and resting it between them. He needed to lighten things up a little. "You're close to Brandi's family. I was surprised her parents weren't at the wedding."

"Yeah. They're out of town on business and don't get back until tomorrow. I guess they couldn't change their plans."

"They're cutting it close to make it to Ian and Brandi's wedding."

"That's the way they are. Very busy people, but you can count on them to be there for their only daughter."

But not for their daughter's best friend who considered them more family than her own. He heard the unspoken words loud and clear. One thing was certain. He needed to show Katie how much he valued and cared about her. "There's one thing I'm still trying to understand. Why didn't you have a single friend other than Brandi at our wedding?"

"What's with all the questions?"

He shrugged. "Call me curious."

She closed her eyes for a moment then opened them and turned to face him. Clear blues eyes stared back at him. "If you must know, no one I invited from my art classes showed, and I don't have any close friends besides Brandi—at least no one that I would invite to my wedding. Happy?"

"No." Not even close. "But I think it's time I let you get some sleep. You're kind of cranky." He got off her bed.

A tiny smile touched her lips. "I'm entitled. It's been

quite a day, and it's my birthday." She climbed from beneath the sheets and walked him to her door—she probably wanted to lock it.

"Why didn't you tell me it was your birthday?"

She shrugged.

He stopped at the threshold. His eyes roamed her body, taking in the curves she usually kept hidden. He touched a hand to her cheek. His wife was beautiful, but something told him no one had ever told her that before. His pastor's words hit him right then—court your wife, until you both fall in love. "You are so beautiful," he leaned close and whispered in her ear before pulling away.

Her eyes widened. "Thank you." She wrapped her arms around her middle.

Maybe his pastor had been right, because at this moment, he did not want to spend his honeymoon night alone. He definitely needed to follow his pastor's advice.

Katie cleared her throat, pulling him from his thoughts. "I thought you were leaving?"

"I am." He nodded. "Happy birthday." He placed a soft kiss on her cheek. "Sweet dreams, Katie." He slipped out the door before she could respond. He had a lot of work to do to court his wife and get past the wall that seemed to be holding her hostage.

12

Katie slipped into her favorite pair of jeans, a pastel pink tank, and then her favorite plaid, pink flannel. Today was the first day of their honeymoon. Ray said they'd be doing something outdoors, so she'd dressed with comfort in mind. She glanced at the clock beside her bed—seven thirty. Her stomach growled. She'd been so nervous all day yesterday; she'd eaten very little, and now she was starving.

A knock on her bedroom door brought a smile to her lips—Ray. Although she'd been a little annoyed with all his questions last night, she welcomed his company. She padded to the door still wearing her favorite pig-faced slippers that Brandi had given her for Christmas and pulled the door open. She caught her breath.

Ray held a large, round tray topped with two covered plates, two goblets filled with orange juice, and a center vase holding a red rose that completed the presentation. "Room service."

"Good morning. Come in." She stepped aside. "I

don't have a table, but we can eat on the bed, I guess."

He grinned. "I've got everything covered." He set the tray on the bed then walked out. A moment later he returned. "It's not fancy, but with a tablecloth I figured it would work." He carried in a small, metal bistro table. "Be right back." He returned with two fancy metal folding chairs that matched the table—one in each hand, and a white cloth draped over his arm.

"You thought of everything. How did you do all of this?"

"The table and chairs were in the garage. The tablecloth is from my mom and…"

He had to bring her up. Suddenly she lost her appetite.

"What? I thought you'd like it. Your room needs a nice place for having coffee and reading the paper. Scratch the coffee, but you know what I mean."

She plastered on a smile. "Thank you." He was right. The table set fit perfectly into her room and gave it a homey feel. "But let's not use the tablecloth. I wouldn't want to accidentally spill anything on it." The last thing Katie needed was to be blamed for ruining something of his mother's.

"I hadn't thought of that. But don't worry." He spread it over the table. "We can use it for now and pick up another one when we're out today."

"Okay. Thank you."

He added the vase with the rose to the center and brought over their meals while she set up the chairs.

"I can't believe you went to this much trouble."

"It was no trouble." He took the covers off the plates with a flourish. "Scrambled eggs, bacon, and fresh peach slices. I make better eggs than pancakes."

"It looks delicious." She'd done the grocery shopping so didn't worry about the gluten factor. She sat and waited for him to join her.

He reached for her hand. "Do you mind if I bless the food?"

She shook her head.

"Lord, I thank You for Katie. Please bless our lives together and this food. Amen." He released her hand and unwrapped silverware from a white cloth napkin. "Eat up. We have a full day ahead."

He'd asked the Lord to bless their lives together. Hope filled her that they might, indeed, have a love-filled marriage one day. But then his mother's words hit her again, and the idea went back to a fantasy. How could a woman like that have such great kids? Then again, her own parents weren't the gems of society, and she'd turned out all right for the most part.

Ray scarfed down his meal and guzzled the juice.

"No coffee?"

He grinned. "I had a cup about an hour ago. Since you don't drink it, I didn't make more."

"You're a nice guy, Ray." She propped her elbows on the table, entwined her fingers and rested her chin on them. "What are we doing today?"

He lifted a brow and relaxed back. "That's up to you. I mentioned canoeing, sailing, and hiking last night, but I read in the paper this morning that the tulip festival is going on. We could drive up to Mt Vernon and check it out if you'd like. You didn't seem overly excited about my other suggestions."

"I enjoy flowers. That could be fun. What about the zoo afterward? We could pick up Emily after lunch and take her with us."

"You want to go to the zoo for our honeymoon?"

She giggled. "I like animals. Besides, I thought this wasn't our honeymoon." They needed to find something to do that Emily would enjoy since Ray had told her he'd pick her up today.

"Animals and flowers." His face brightened. "I like it. But let's do the zoo another day. I called Emily earlier and told her today wasn't going to work out after all since our friends are getting married tomorrow, and we have a lot to do. For a little tike, she understood better than I expected."

Katie gasped. "I can't believe I forgot about Brandi's wedding! Even after she spent all day yesterday helping me. I'm the worst friend ever."

He reached out and rested his hand over hers. "No, you're the second-worst friend. I forgot as well, or I would never have told Emily she could join us."

Katie chuckled. "We are quite the pair. Maybe we're a match made in heaven, after all."

Ray raised a brow. "I have a feeling you're more correct than you realize. I never would have gone through with this if I didn't sense the Lord's blessing on us."

She'd truly married a godly man. Too bad her

mother hadn't. She cringed.

"What's wrong?" His grip tightened slightly.

"I still need to figure out what to do about my mom."

"What do you mean?"

"I know I agreed to meet her for the next two weeks, but I'm not sure to what end."

"You catch up. Get some questions answered."

"I guess that's a start, but let's not talk about her." This was the first day of the rest of their lives together, and she wanted it to be special.

"Eat up. Breakfast is getting cold." Ray removed his hand from hers.

She tried the eggs and grinned. How was it the man cooked so well and still wasted money going out to eat every Friday? Maybe he could only cook eggs. That would get boring. Even though she enjoyed cooking, she had to admit, it was nice having someone else take over. She could get used to being pampered, but it wouldn't be a regular occurrence since part of her job description was to cook. Wait, was she still being paid to take care of Emily and cook and clean? She didn't dare ask.

"You look deep in thought. The food okay?"

"It's delicious. I was thinking about how things will be different now that we're married."

A hopeful look lit his eyes.

"Like my relationship with Emily, for example, is different now that I'm her aunt."

"Oh. Right."

Was that disappointment in his voice?

"I think she's thought of you as an aunt for a while now since you and Renee were friends."

She shrugged. "Maybe." He sure couldn't take a hint. But she refused to come out and ask if she was still being paid for her services. Stay-at-home spouses didn't get paid, so she imagined she wouldn't. She shook off the thought—it was ridiculous to let her mind go there. They were on their honeymoon, and Ray was clearly trying to make their day memorable. She quickly finished eating. "Thank you for this wonderful meal. It was a nice way to begin the day."

"You're welcome." He stood. "I'll take this downstairs and clean up. I thought we could leave in about thirty minutes. Does that work for you?"

"Sure. Would you like help?"

"Not necessary. See you in a bit." He stacked everything onto the tray, and before she realized his intent, he placed a quick kiss on her cheek. "You look lovely this morning, in case I forgot to mention it. The slippers are a nice touch." He winked then left her room.

Ray stood at the bottom of the stairs in his house holding a bouquet of balloons. Thankfully, the grocery store had a florist that opened early and was able to put it together for him.

Katie trotted down the stairs and froze as soon as her gaze slammed into the balloons. "Whoa!"

"Happy belated birthday! I thought after we go to the tulip festival we could find a bakery and celebrate with a slice of cake."

"Or a cupcake." Her eyes twinkled as she eased down the remaining stairs. "I love the balloons. Thank you. I didn't tell you it was my birthday so you'd—"

He raised a hand, cutting off her words. "I believe birthdays are meant to be celebrated. Don't spoil my fun." He had a sudden idea. It probably wouldn't work to go to Pike's Place until after Ian and Brandi's wedding and they'd probably need to take Emily along, but he'd make it work. Courting his wife was going to be more fun than he had realized.

She pressed her lips together and nodded.

"Good. Now that we understand each other." He handed her the balloons anchored with a small decorative sandbag.

She set them on the bottom stair. "I'll take them to my room later. Shouldn't we get a move on if we're going to have time for everything?"

He bowed from the waist then offered his arm.

Giggling, she slid her hand around his bicep.

His heart soared. Maybe his mom hadn't done as much damage as he'd thought. Talk about a relief.

An hour later, they walked along rows of colorful tulips. He pulled out his cell phone and snapped several pictures of his wife among the flowers. Before they left, he bought several stems then they headed back to Seattle.

Katie sighed from her side of the car. "That was nice."

He grinned and slid a glance her direction. "I agree.

145

Why haven't we ever done anything like that before?"

"Because you are a workaholic, and I was too intimidated by you."

He jerked his head back. "For real?"

"Yes, but don't worry." She grinned. "I've warmed up to you now."

Thinking about it, her admission made sense. She had rarely spoken in his presence before that night at the diner. "What changed?"

"You needed me more than I needed to protect myself."

"From me?"

"Not necessarily. More from myself."

He shook his head. "I don't follow."

She took a breath and let it out slowly. "I had a crush on you, and I knew you didn't feel the same way. I didn't want to do or say anything to embarrass myself. It became a habit to stay quiet around you. I'm not sure what got into me that night at the diner."

He glanced her way as he changed lanes to exit I-5. Katie's face was bright red. "I had no idea. I wish I'd known." He thought back over the past couple of years and couldn't recall a single hint she'd dropped about her feelings.

"Would it have made a difference?"

"It's possible." He wanted to say yes, but he'd been wrapped up in work and his charity. He hadn't had time for anything more than a once-in-a-while casual date. Then again, if the Katie he'd come to know over the past several weeks had made an appearance back then, he would have definitely noticed her. "I wish I hadn't been so clueless." Maybe they would have fallen in love a long time ago and not be in the situation they'd found themselves in now.

She laughed. "I'm glad you were. I wasn't ready for you to notice me."

"Why's that?" He raised a brow as he glanced her direction.

She only shrugged.

He pulled up to the gluten free bakery Hailey had recommended. "Here we are. I hear they serve lunch and cupcakes."

"Sounds good to me." She shot him a shy look.

Uh-oh. Had their conversation put that expression of uncertainty on her face? He scrambled around to the passenger door and opened it for her. When she got out, he wrapped his warm hand around her cold one and gave it a gentle squeeze.

They placed their orders then sat by a window. Katie laced her fingers on the table in front of her and stared down at them. "Where did you find my ring? It looks vintage, and it's gorgeous."

He grinned—finally! "I bought it from your buddy at the pawn shop where we purchased mine."

"No way!" She raised her hand and studied the ring at different angles. "It's remarkable. Thank you. I don't know how you managed to find the perfect ring, but you did."

"It wasn't easy, but once I realized you wouldn't be happy with a traditional wedding set, I went back to the pawn shop. The minute I saw that ring, I knew it was the one." Much like he now knew, without a doubt, she was the one for him. She'd admitted having a crush on him—at least she did at one time. Did she still feel the same way? He wasn't ready to go there yet. What they had was still too new—a work in progress for sure.

13

Monday evening, Katie held tightly to Emily's hand as they walked the distance from the community center to the athletic club. She was so nervous her entire body trembled. Why had she ever agreed to meet her mom?

She pulled open the door and strode inside.

Tasha smiled. "He's in his office."

"Thanks." She took the stairs carefully with Emily as the little girl led with the same foot up each stair.

The door at the top opened, and Ray stood there with a silly grin on his face.

"What?" She frowned. It had been a long day, and she was having second thoughts about meeting her mom.

"Nothing. Can't a man enjoy watching his family?"

"I suppose." Although she didn't have personal experience with that—until now.

Ray stepped aside, allowing them to enter. He scooped Emily into his arms and planted a kiss on her forehead. "How was your day, munchkin?"

"Good."

"I'll take the bus home." Katie turned back toward the stairs.

"We'll wait," Ray said. "You can ride home with us."

"Emily's hungry."

"I have snacks here. Don't worry." He set Emily down and walked over to Katie. He placed a hand on each of her shoulders. "It's going to be okay."

"How do you know?"

"Because you're strong, and I have faith in you."

"You have more faith in me than I do."

He pulled her into his arms and held her for several seconds. She rested her head against his chest, his heart beating a steady rhythm. She wrapped her arms around his waist. Tension rolled off her. "I feel better now. Thank you."

"Any time." He released her. "How about if we walk you there?"

"I should do this on my own."

"You will."

"Okay." Having them walk with her would be nice. But she needed to meet Mom alone this time. As a grown woman, she shouldn't allow anyone to hold her hand while she talked with her mother.

They marched down the stairs and out onto the sidewalk.

Emily walked between them, holding each of their hands. "Can we get ice cream?"

"No," Ray said. "You won't want dinner if you eat ice cream right now."

"Boo." Her bottom lip protruded.

Katie almost laughed but didn't want to encourage Emily's attitude. "I have a yummy dinner planned. You won't want to be too full."

"What is it?" Emily asked.

Katie glanced at Ray.

He nodded.

"Homemade pizza! You get to make your own."

"Really?" Emily's face lit.

"Yes." Katie had been reading up on ways to get children to eat healthy. One of the suggestions was getting kids involved in cooking their meals. She smiled to herself—not that pizza was a great food, but she had healthy toppings prepared, so it would be nutritious.

"I like pizza."

They stopped outside the Starbucks. "Good. I'll meet you back at The Ring in a little while, okay?"

Emily nodded.

Ray took her hand. "You'll be fine."

"Thanks." She took a bracing breath, squared her shoulders, and marched inside. Her mother sat in the back corner. Somehow she hadn't pictured her mom as someone who would look so put together, but looking at her now, she'd never know the past they'd shared. Her red hair cascaded to her shoulders in perfect waves, and her clothes fit perfectly.

Her mother raised a hand when she spotted her.

Katie nodded then detoured to the counter to order

a non-coffee beverage. A few minutes later, she carried her drink to the table and sat across from the woman who'd abandoned her.

"I was afraid you might not show," her mom said.

"It was tempting." Katie stuffed a straw into her drink and took a long draw. "What are you hoping to gain from this?"

"Forgiveness."

Relief surged through Katie. Although hurt immeasurably by her mother's actions, she had long ago forgiven her. "Done."

"Just like that?" Confusion filled her mom's face.

"Not even. It took years to come to that point, but I did. I realized you weren't worth all the pain not forgiving you caused me."

Her mom jerked her head back as if slapped. "That wasn't very nice."

Remorse immediately struck Katie. "You're right. I should have worded that differently. What I was trying to say was that holding onto the anger and not forgiving was toxic to me. It wasn't worth the harm it was doing to me both emotionally and physically. So, one day, I decided enough was enough."

"You made the decision to forgive me and that was the end of it?"

"Not exactly. That was the beginning of the process."

Mom nodded. "You're wise beyond your years."

"Sink or swim as they say. I got thrown into the deep end of the pool without a life preserver when you left."

Mom's eyes watered. "I'd hoped your father would change after I left."

"Seriously? Even after he threatened you? You actually believed he'd change?"

Mom grabbed a napkin and wiped trailing tears from her face. "I wish I was as strong and wise as you are, Katie. I don't know how you turned out so well considering everything."

"It certainly wasn't thanks to you." Katie winced. "Sorry, I did it again. Seeing you has stirred up feelings I thought I was long past. Maybe I still need to work on my anger."

"It's okay. I deserve it."

Katie shrugged. She did not want to be here. She'd made the choice to forgive her parents some time ago, but showing her mom respect was difficult after what she'd done. "I agreed to meet with you, not because I want to renew a relationship with you, but because I was hoping for answers. I have the why for your disappearance and the how. I also know why you waited so long to find me."

"But…" Mom pressed her lips together.

"Now I'd like to know some simple things like, do I have any half siblings, do you have any genetic health issues—that kind of stuff."

Relief filled her mom's eyes. "I never remarried. You don't have any siblings, and other than tendinitis, I'm perfectly healthy. Although my mom had diabetes."

"Good to know. Thank you." Now what? She checked the time on her cell phone. "I should get going."

She pushed back and stood.

Her mom's gaze landed on Katie's left hand. "Did you get married since I last saw you, or is that your engagement ring?"

Katie stuffed her hand into her pocket. "I'm married."

Her mom frowned. "I wish you hadn't done that. You're so young. I don't want you making the same mistakes I did."

"That won't happen. Ray is a good man, and I trust him." At least she trusted him as much as she could. Complete trust seemed to be impossible.

Mom's eyes narrowed. "No man can be trusted. I hope you don't regret your decision."

Me, too. "I won't. Per our agreement, I'll see you here the same time next week."

"Right. Are you sure you can't stay for a bit?"

"Why?" She didn't want to hurt her mother, but she had nothing to say to her. What was the point of pretending?

A shadow crossed her mom's eyes. "I don't know. I'll see you next week."

Katie turned and left without looking back. So many feelings coursed through her: unease, irritation that her mother thought Ray was a bad guy simply because he was a man, sadness that her mom had lived such a hard life, and relief that she'd only have to see her mom once more before she'd be able to close the door on her forever if she wanted to. Did she want to though? She kind of felt bad for her mom. Then again, everyone had to live with their own choices. Katie knew that firsthand.

14

From the kitchen, Ray watched Katie and Emily as they sat on the couch reading. The homemade pizza had been a success, and now he hoped his niece would settle down so she'd go to sleep soon. Ever since Katie had moved in, he looked forward to visiting with her in the evenings.

Since Emily had gotten off schedule at his mom's, last night had not gone well. It had been quite the challenge to get her to bed. He finished wiping down the counter, tossed the rag into the sink, then went and sat on the other side of Emily. She snuggled into his side and yawned —a good sign.

Katie's soft voice lilted as she read the last page in the book. "The end." She closed the cover. "Time for bed, little miss."

"I want Uncle Ray to tuck me in." She climbed into his lap and wrapped her arms around his neck. Ten minutes later his niece was snug in bed. Anticipation gripped him—he could finally have alone time with

Katie. He hadn't been able to read her after she'd visited with her mom, and he was anxious to know how it went. Halfway down the stairs, he realized the house was encased in darkness. Had Katie gone to bed early?

He pivoted and retraced his steps then walked to the end of the hall. Sure enough, her bedroom door was closed. A light shone beneath it. Should he give her space or knock? She hadn't sought out his company even once since moving in. Maybe he was pushing her too hard; then again, she was so reserved if he didn't push, they'd never get to know one another.

Her door swung open, and she surged out with her focus on her phone.

"Hi," he said softly, not wanting to wake Emily.

She froze and looked up. "Oh. I didn't realize you were finished with Emily already. That was fast."

"Yes. She was worn out."

A smile touched her lips. "I know the feeling. What are you doing hanging out in the hallway?"

"I was debating whether I should knock on your door or not."

She raised a brow. "You'd dare to enter my room without hot chocolate or food." She shot him a teasing grin.

He snapped his fingers. "I knew I was forgetting something. I'll be right back."

She stepped forward and tugged on his arm. "I was only kidding. You're always welcome to visit if my light is on. I just got a text from Brandi, and I was coming to wait outside Emily's room for you."

"What'd she say?" It didn't escape him that they still stood in the hallway. He'd invite her into his room, but for whatever reason, it didn't seem appropriate. "We could go downstairs and talk."

She shook her head. "No. Come see what I did with the table set you brought in. It's cozy." She turned and ambled into her room. "What do you think?"

He chuckled. "You *girlyfied* it." White frilly pillows adorned the chairs, and a simple matching tablecloth covered the table. "It's nice in a girly kind of way." He made a silly face. "If you like frou-frou, that is."

She playfully punched his shoulder. "It is a girl's room. Have a seat. I had it all in a box in the garage, so it was a cinch to make it more my style." She sat in the chair furthest away, leaving him the closest. "Brandi said they had an uneventful flight and are settled in at the hotel."

"I still can't believe they're honeymooning in London when they're going to be living there."

"I know, but Ian starts work next week, and they needed time to find a flat and get settled."

He raised a brow. "Listen to you. A flat, huh? No apartments in London."

She chuckled. "I didn't realize what a tease you are. Why is that?"

He shrugged. "I don't know." Katie hadn't seemed open to teasing. She was always so serious that he hadn't known how she'd take it. Now that he'd gotten to know her, he realized that when she did joke, it was often a defense mechanism for uncomfortable situations.

So…why had she been uncomfortable around him? "Maybe it's the change in our relationship. You're more easygoing now."

"I am?"

He nodded. "What changed?"

She was quiet for a moment then softly said, "Everything."

Yes, everything had changed. In a matter of weeks both of their lives had been turned upside down. "Good point. Will you tell me about your meeting with your mom?"

"There's not much to tell. She wanted forgiveness, and I gave it to her. We agreed to meet once more." Her gaze slammed into his. "I forgot to check with you to make sure you could watch Emily."

"I'm free. When you first set this up with your mom, I cleared my schedule."

"You mean you normally have plans on Mondays?" Her voice hitched.

He chuckled, though it wasn't funny. "I used to be busy all the time. I probably worked fifty to sixty hours a week. I've made adjustments since Emily became a constant in my life. Plus, there's you." He dipped his head. He'd gone out of his way to make time for Katie.

"I feel bad that I've caused you to change your schedule. Although, no one should work that much. You make me look like a complete slacker." Her shoulders sagged ever so slightly. "You know what? It's fine if Emily joins us. I'll bring her with me. I doubt we'll be long."

"You're sure?" He wasn't crazy about Emily being in the company of Katie's mom. Her mother might get some grandiose idea of wanting to be a grandmother, and they didn't need another change in their lives.

"Yes. But it doesn't seem like you think it's a good idea."

"I have reservations."

"I can cancel," Katie said. "I've found out everything I wanted, so it's not a big deal."

"No. You should meet with your mom like you agreed."

"Ray, I don't want you altering your life for me. If you would have been working, then that's what you should be doing."

He shook his head. "Make up your mind." He grinned. "One minute I work too much, and the next, you want me working overtime."

She flashed an embarrassed grin. "Sorry."

"Don't worry about my schedule. I can make this work and still get in a couple extra hours of paperwork."

"How?"

"I'll see if Hailey can take her."

"Are you sure that's a good idea? Your mom and Hailey have had her a lot these past several days since we were supposed to be honeymooning."

"Emily understands and so does my mom and sister. My family loves having her." Though time together had been sparse because of Ian and Brandi's rehearsal and wedding, they'd had a good time nonetheless. He felt like they'd grown closer in the process.

"Okay. We can ask, but if she says no, then we need to come up with a Plan B."

"I'm sure it'll be fine. Speaking of our pseudo-honeymoon. Did you enjoy it?'

Her gaze shot to his and held for a moment. "Yes. It was fun."

He studied her light blue eyes. There was something there he hadn't noticed before—desire? He sucked in a breath.

"What are you thinking?" she asked softly.

"I'm thinking about how much I've grown to care about you in a very short amount of time."

Her eyes widened, but she remained silent. Had he misread her?

She stood and walked to the window, her back turned to him. "I'm glad."

"Really? It doesn't scare you?" He followed and stood behind her. The sky shone clear with a nearly full moon. He rested his hands on her shoulders and gently kneaded the knotted muscles.

"That feels so good." She leaned into him slightly. "Your feelings don't scare me." She turned, causing his hands to drop. "In fact, I think I feel the same way, or I never would have married you."

This was news. A zip of electricity shot through him.

"I care about you, and I love Emily. I'd do anything for her." Sincerity shown in her eyes.

As fast as the excitement came, it vanished. Concern hit him. Did she only marry him to provide a mother figure for his niece? No. She said she cared about him, too. But was it the kind of caring a woman has for the man she loves or something different?

"What?" Concern filled her eyes as she gazed into his. "Did I say something wrong?"

"Not at all. I feel the same for my niece. I want the best for her." Talk about a shift. A few moments ago, he thought they were well on their way to falling in love, especially since she'd admitted to having a crush on him. Confusion and uncertainty enveloped him. He didn't want to read too much into her comment. He should ask for clarification, but it was getting late. It would keep for another conversation. "I better try to sleep. Good night, Katie."

Her lips tipped down. "Okay. Sleep well."

"Where are we going?" Katie trotted alongside Ray, who had Emily on his shoulders.

A grin tipped his lips. "It's a surprise."

Downtown Seattle had gotten off to a lazy Saturday morning. They rounded a corner, and she gasped. Pike Place Market loomed ahead. She should have figured this is where he was taking them. They'd been talking last night at dinner about the fishmongers who threw fish. Katie had been fascinated by his description.

Ray slowed his pace. "Remember how I told you about the flying fish, Emily?"

"Yep." She patted the top of his head from her perch.

"Well look." He pointed to the display of halibut and the small crowd gathered around.

A man shouted something and then tossed the fish probably twenty feet to someone behind the counter who caught it in a piece of what looked like freezer paper.

Emily clapped her hands. "Will he do it again, Uncle Ray?"

"When someone else buys a fish, he will."

Katie grinned at the wonder in the child's eyes that probably matched her own. She'd only been here once, several years ago. Her focus shifted to the vast display of cut flowers for sale, reminding her of the tulips Ray had purchased for her on their "honeymoon" last week. Katie's insides warmed at the memory.

If she hadn't been in love with Ray already, she surely would be now. What surprised her the most was his thoughtful concern for her wellbeing and happiness. But it wasn't like he loved her back. Yes, he said he cared for her, but that wasn't love—was it? She could only hope.

She wanted to share the kind of love their friends had, but for now, his kindness was enough. She nibbled her bottom lip. She'd thought he was on his way there, but other than being attentive to her, he'd not shown any sign of being a man in love. What if he never loved her back?

15

Monday evening, Emily grasped Katie's hand and skipped alongside her as they headed down the block toward The Ring. "That was fun."

"I'm glad you enjoyed the arts and crafts. You behaved well."

"Mommy says that little girls should always behave in public."

Katie grinned. "She was right. Are you looking forward to seeing your Aunt Hailey soon?"

She nodded. "I love Aunt Hailey."

Katie breathed a little easier knowing Emily would be content. She should have had Hailey meet them at the community center since the final visit with her mom would be relatively quick, but meeting her at The Ring wasn't that much different since they were on the same block.

Hailey approached from the opposite direction and waved. "How's my favorite niece?" she called out.

Emily giggled and tugged her hand free then raced

to her aunt.

Hailey wrapped her in a bear hug and stood with the child in her arms. She waited for Katie to catch up. "I thought we'd hang out in Ray's office and play a game. I brought one over the last time I was here for times like this."

"Good thinking. I don't expect to be long."

"Take your time," Hailey said before heading into the gym.

Katie took a bracing breath, squared her shoulders, then marched to the crosswalk. Her palms sweated. Why was she so nervous? Her mom wasn't a threat.

She walked into the shop and quickly spotted her mother. An expectant look filled her eyes. What was she up to?

Katie approached the table. "Hi."

She wouldn't bother with a drink today. The sooner she could leave the better, and a drink would slow her down.

Mom smiled. "Hi yourself. Have a seat."

Katie took the chair across the table. "Did you have a nice week?" She may not desire a relationship, or completely trust her mother, but she would be nice.

"It was long. You?"

"Mine flew." Being married to Ray and taking care of Emily had turned her life into a whirlwind. She'd barely had time to catch her breath. A large medium-sized manila envelope sat on the table piquing her curiosity. "Why was your week so long?"

"Mostly because I was anxious for our meeting. I

don't want our visits to end. I could come to Seattle from time to time. It would be nice for us to have a fresh start. Don't you think?"

"If it were possible to wipe away my memories, I would agree, but I don't think a fresh start is possible. There's too much baggage."

Mom's face drooped. "There doesn't have to be. You said you've forgiven me. I thought we could build on that. You're my baby girl, and I've missed you."

Katie swallowed the lump that had formed in her throat. Having a mother again would be a dream come true, but what if once her mother got to know her, she took off like last time? Katie couldn't take that kind of pain again. But still, her heart hurt for all her mom had been through. The pain her rotten dad had caused them both—at least they had that in common. But seeing her…having Mom in her life again? "I think we need to take baby steps. Do you e-mail?" She could set up an account to use only with her mom. That way if things got weird all she had to do was close it.

"I do."

"Maybe that would be the best way to move forward."

"E-mailing each other?" Mom frowned. "I wanted you to be a part of my life again. I wanted us to be a real family."

"I think it might be too late for that." She clenched her hands together in her lap. Why did this have to be so difficult? Not having parents in her life had been so much easier than this. "E-mailing is the best I can do for now."

Mom seemed to contemplate her words then squared her shoulders and raised her chin ever so slightly. "Then that's what we'll do. But first I have something for you." She slid the envelope across the table.

"What is it?" Her hand shook as she grasped it.

"I never told you this because you were too young, but you're old enough now, and you're under no delusions about your father. He cheated on me more than once. I don't want you to go through what I did. I had your husband followed this past week."

Anger filled her. "Why? Ray is nothing like Dad." Katie's voice raised a notch, and several people looked in their direction.

"I hope you're right, but I needed to see what kind of man you married. Trust me. You'll want to see those pictures."

Katie's stomach dropped. Could she have been wrong about Ray? She dropped the envelope onto the table. Ray was a good man. Mom had to be mistaken. He would never do anything to hurt her. So why was she terrified to know what pictures were inside the envelope?

Her mother pulled a pad of paper and a pen from her purse. She scribbled something down, tore off the sheet, then handed it to Katie. "When you're ready, that's my e-mail. I love you, Katie." She stood. "I hope to hear from you soon." Without a backward glance, her mom marched away and out the door.

Katie shook her head and focused on the envelope.

Did she really want to know what was inside? She knew in her heart that Ray was a good man, so whatever her mom thought she had on him had to be a mistake.

She stuffed it into her purse. The pictures would keep. Emily needed dinner and was depending on her.

Ray draped his arm across the back of the couch and rested his hand on Katie's shoulder. "It's finally just us."

Katie snuggled her head against his shoulder.

He could get used to evenings like this. "You never said how it went with your mom."

Katie sighed. "She gave me her e-mail address."

"That's not necessarily a bad thing, is it? After all, she is your mother."

"And she doesn't like you, so I wouldn't work too hard at defending her."

He frowned. "She doesn't know me."

"You're a man and my husband. Apparently, that's enough."

He shifted. It wasn't fair. But not much was where Katie's family was concerned. "You think I could win her over?"

"Of course you could, given time, but you don't have that. Remember, she and I aren't meeting anymore."

"Right." He frowned. It shouldn't matter if her mother didn't like him, but it did. Now he knew how Katie felt regarding his mom.

Katie stilled beside him. The clock on the wall

ticked away the seconds. "Is there anything I should know about you?" Her voice was barely above a whisper.

"Hmm. I think you know all there is to know. Why do you ask?" The serious look on her face caused him to tense.

She shrugged. "We're married. I just thought…that is, you can tell me anything. Okay?"

"I appreciate that. Where's this coming from?"

"Something my mother said. It's no biggie."

"It feels important." He frowned. What wasn't she saying?

"Don't worry. She has a way of getting in my head. I'm sorry I worried you."

"Okay. Talking goes both ways. You can talk to me about anything, too."

"Thanks."

"So, is there anything you want to talk about? Anything I should know?"

She pressed her lips together as if in deep thought. "Grace is my middle name."

"That's Hailey's nickname. Grace suits you. I like it." He tried to smile, but suspected he failed. "Anything else?"

"Nope."

He knew something was off with her, but clearly, she wasn't going to talk. Why didn't she trust him?

16

Katie sat at the table in her bedroom and stared at the envelope. She'd had it for a week and had yet to open it. Sitting here and wondering about it had become a late-night ritual. It was time. Not knowing the contents had become worse than facing the pictures.

She grabbed the manila envelope in one hand and opened the top. "Here goes nothing." Reaching her fingers inside, she grasped the contents and pulled them out. She held three pictures in front of her and peered at the first. Ray sat in a booth at the breakfast place he'd taken her. Relief washed over her. She knew he enjoyed going there. Talk about overreacting. She flipped to the next photo and stilled. A woman sat close beside him. The picture was dated four days after their wedding.

She looked closer at the picture and studied the woman's profile. Something about her was familiar. Some detective her mom hired. What was Katie supposed to do with this if she couldn't identify the woman? For all she knew he could be there on business—if only she could see the mystery woman's face. Katie flipped the third and final picture and gasped.

They were standing and Ray was hugging her.

Katie's face heated, and her heart raced. She dropped the photos onto the table and pushed back. There had to be a good explanation. Ray didn't go around hugging women. She should march to his room right now and show him the pictures.

She thrust the photos into the envelope and stood with leaded feet. They'd been living a fairytale. A couple didn't just marry on a whim and live happily ever after—especially two people in their situation. Ray only claimed to care for her. He never said he loved her. It was time to face reality. Her husband, though a good man, would never truly be the husband she'd hoped for.

A scream wrenched her from her thoughts. "Emily?" She bolted to her bedroom door and raced into the hall.

Ray stood there with a puzzled look on his face as if he wasn't sure what he'd heard.

The scream sliced the air again. His face paled. He spun and ran the short distance to Emily's room then flipped on the light.

Emily tossed in her bed mumbling.

"What's wrong with her?" Ray went to her bedside and rested a hand on her forehead. "Do you think she's sick?"

Katie sat on the other side of the bed and reached for the little girl's hand. "Emily, sweetie. Wake up." She glanced across the bed at Ray. "I think she's having a bad dream."

Relief covered Ray's face then he frowned.

Emily's eyes sprung open. She jumped then sat up and threw herself into Katie's arms. Soft sobs filled the quiet room. Katie's eyes burned, and she blinked rapidly. She would not cry.

Ray eased onto the other side of Emily's bed. "What's the matter, munchkin? Did you have a bad dream?"

Emily sniffled and turned her face to look at her uncle.

"Do you want to talk about it?" Ray asked.

"No. Can you and Aunt Katie sleep in my bed with me tonight?"

"Your bed isn't big enough for the three of us." He rubbed her back.

Fresh tears streamed down Emily's cheeks.

Katie's heart wrenched. "How about I stay here for a bit with you?"

"Really?" Emily's voice wobbled.

"Mm-hmm." Katie nodded as she stroked the child's hair away from her face.

"Thanks." Her eyes brightened a little as she scooted over to make room.

Either the child was a master manipulator or she recovered quickly.

Ray chuckled. "Sleep well."

"Thanks. You, too. Hopefully, she won't have any more nightmares." Katie waited for Ray to leave the room then snuggled next to her niece. "I'll pray that you don't have more bad dreams."

"Okay. Thank you. My mommy and daddy used to do that, too. Daddy said to think happy thoughts."

"That's a great idea." Katie pulled the bedding up to Emily's neck. "Lord, please be with Your child as she sleeps. Please fill her dreams with happiness. Amen."

Emily's body relaxed beside hers, and soft snores followed. Katie slipped from the bed and tiptoed to the door. She startled when she spotted Ray pacing the space between their rooms.

He looked her direction and rushed toward her. "How is she?"

"Sleeping peacefully."

"That's a relief. Thank you."

Katie nodded. She was going to have her own nightmares if she didn't show Ray those photos. "We need to talk."

His brow scrunched. "Okay."

She passed him and led the way to her room, grabbing the envelope before sitting at the bistro table.

Ray sat across from her. "What do you have there?"

"Remember when I told you my mom doesn't like you?"

He nodded.

"Well, she had you followed."

His jaw dropped open for a moment before he clamped it shut. "Go on."

She pulled the photographs from the envelope and slid them his direction. "I trust you, Ray, but I am curious who the woman is that you're hugging. It's difficult to tell from the angle of the picture."

He picked up the photo then set it down. "It's Kari White, our wedding photographer. We met so she could give me the flash drive with the pictures from our wedding. She had a special print made as a gift to us and wanted to deliver it in person."

Sudden tears pricked at Katie's eyes. She never should have let her mother get into her head. "That was nice of her. Where's the picture? I'd love to see photo."

He grinned. "I'm having it framed. I plan to hang it above the mantel. I was going to surprise you."

"I'm sorry your surprise is spoiled."

He shrugged. "It's okay. Is this the reason you've been acting a little off for the past week?"

She shrugged. "Maybe. I knew I could trust you, but I guess I still had a shadow of doubt that made me afraid to look inside the envelope."

"Why were you afraid?"

"My mother suggested you were cheating on me. I didn't want it to be true, because I like what we have growing between us. If she'd been right, then this would have ended. I'm really glad you're the man I thought you were."

He placed his hands on the tabletop palms up. She placed hers in his.

"I would never do that to you—to us."

She nodded, unwilling to trust her voice. He might not have said the words, but this sure felt like love.

Ray yawned as he strode into The Ring. He'd tossed and

turned all night after his conversation with Katie. Something had changed between them last night, and he wasn't entirely sure how to proceed.

"Good morning, boss." Tasha flashed a wide smile.

He nodded. "Is Rusty downstairs?"

"He is. Everything okay?"

"Yes. Thanks." He detoured to the stairs leading down to the boxing ring where two women were sparring. Rusty held a bag as one of their regulars pummeled it. Ray waited off to the side. Maybe this was a mistake. Rusty didn't need to know his personal problems. Then again he'd always been there for him in the past. He knew he could trust the man.

A short time later, Rusty sauntered his direction. "How's it going?" He reached out his hand.

Ray took it and gave him a firm handshake. "Not bad." He nodded toward the trainer's office. "Does that offer to talk still stand?"

"Always." They headed into Rusty's office, and Ray closed the door. Rusty perched sideways off the corner of his desk. "What's on your mind?"

"Katie." He sat in a leather chair that dated back to the fifties or sixties, which was still in surprisingly good condition.

The trainer chuckled. "I thought maybe."

"You were married for a long time."

He nodded. "Not long enough. But thirty-five years is long to most people. What seems to be the problem?"

"Not a problem really, but I'm curious about something." He frowned. This was more difficult than he'd expected. He'd always been able to talk easily with Rusty but never about something so personal. He cleared his throat. "I'm going to tell you something that would send tongues wagging all the way to Canada, so…"

"You're asking me to keep my mouth shut." He grinned, showing a full set of slightly crooked teeth. "You don't need to worry about me, son. I'm no gossip."

"I think I knew that, but I needed you to know— this doesn't leave your office."

Rusty's face sobered.

He shared his story with Rusty from start to finish, leaving out nothing.

"That's quite a situation you have yourself in, but what seems to be the trouble?"

"The thing is, I've tried to show her that I care about her, even told her so, but it doesn't seem to be enough." Ray rubbed the back of his neck. "Did you ever tell your wife you loved her?"

"Of course." Rusty sounded indignant.

"I didn't mean to offend you. It's just that I don't ever remember hearing my parents tell one another they loved each other. My family isn't very expressive about our feelings."

Rusty rubbed his chin. "No offense taken. But are you telling me you've never told Katie you love her?"

He nodded and swallowed the lump in his throat.

"You must tell your wife you love her. Daily."

Ray's head dipped. *Daily?* He had a lot to learn about marriage. He stood. "Okay. This has been helpful.

Thanks." He pulled open the door and trudged from the room then up the stairs.

He'd never said those words to a woman before. He'd dated casually, and there had been someone once, but she'd accused him of being emotionally unavailable. Had she really been asking for him to say he loved her? He would only say it if he meant it, and he hadn't then. But Katie…

"Boss, you have messages." She handed him a stack of pink papers.

"No one does voicemail anymore?" He shook his head and took the sticky notes she held out to him. "Thanks. I'll be in my office." Curiosity piqued, he jogged up the stairs. The messages were from his grandfather's attorney, his mother, and Ian. His heart thumped hard. Ian was his best buddy, and he never called. His eyes roamed over the paper looking for a message. It only said to call.

He punched in the number.

"Thanks for calling so fast."

"No problem. What's wrong?"

"Why do you think something's wrong?"

"You never call."

"I couldn't get you off my mind. Is everything okay there?"

"Things are fine."

"You sure? It's not like me to have such a strong feeling to call a person."

"Well actually, I've been struggling with something." Ray glanced toward his office door to make sure it was closed. "I need to tell Katie I love her, and I'm not sure how to."

"Do you love her?"

"It's crazy, but yeah. I think I do. I've never felt this way before." He hadn't realized until now how much he'd miss not having Katie in his life, and it wasn't only because she made his life easier by cooking his meals and taking care of Emily. She was sweet, funny, complex, filled with surprises, and so much more. He'd never imagined falling in love so fast or so completely, but he had. Joy leapt through him.

"You there, Ray?"

"Yeah. Did I miss something?"

Ian chuckled. "Only a long speech on the benefits of romancing your wife and making sure you tell her you love her."

"But what if she doesn't love me back?"

"I shouldn't tell you this, but Brandi told me she thinks Katie has had a crush on you for a long time. I wouldn't be surprised if she's loved you for a while."

"She mentioned something about having a crush on me."

"Then what are you waiting for?"

Ray's face heated. "I hear you. Thanks for the call. Is everything all right on your end?"

"Things here are great. We're settling into life as a married couple and have even made some friends."

"I'm glad. Thanks for the advice. I'll let you go." A sudden idea struck him. He had a lot to do.

17

Katie sat across from Emily in her bedroom. A teapot rested in the center of the child-sized table, covered with the makings for a tea party. "Would you like one lump or two?" She held mini tongs in between her thumb and pointer finger over a tiny dish of sugar lumps.

"Two please." Emily sat prim and proper. "May I have a sandwich also please?"

"Of course. Help yourself."

Emily reached for a crust-free wedge of peanut butter and jelly. Not high-tea fare, but for a four-year-old, it was perfect.

Katie would stick with her bowl of fresh berries doused with whipped cream.

"Mommy and me had tea parties, too. Only she made tea cakes."

Katie grinned. "You had a good mommy." She brought a teacup to her lips.

"I know. Is your mommy good, too?"

Katie stopped with the cup poised mid-air. "She didn't used to be, but she is trying to be now." She'd given her mother a lot of thought over the past several days and had come to the conclusion that she'd been wrong when she said they couldn't have a fresh start.

There was nothing stopping them from moving forward as mother and daughter from where they were now so long as she could accept Ray as Katie's husband and stop trying to find fault with him. Being here with Emily like this made her realize even more what she'd missed by not having her mother in her life. She didn't want to lose out any longer. Granted, her mom would never have put on a tea party, but it wasn't too late to try. She wanted a relationship with her mom, but could she trust her?

"Trying is the first step in doing," Emily said.

Katie grinned. "Yes. It is, isn't it?"

Where had Emily heard that? She was too young to come up with it on her own. Then again, she could very well be wise beyond her years. Especially considering the huge amount of time she spent around adults.

Katie placed the teacup onto its matching saucer. *Trying is the first step.* Although she would never forget her past and the hurt and pain her mom caused, that wasn't a bad thing. Those memories helped form her into the woman she was now and gave her enough caution to use good sense where relationships were concerned.

"I wish I could have a tea party with my mommy. You're so lucky to have a mommy again. And I have you now."

A lump formed in Katie's throat. Emily didn't have a choice whether to see her mom again or not, but Katie did. She didn't want to have any regrets. But she would proceed with caution. "You are a very wise little girl."

"I am?" Emily's face brightened. "Thanks."

Katie tapped her niece's nose. "Eat up."

Emily giggled. "You're wise, too, Aunt Katie." She took a big bite of her sandwich and chewed. A smile lit her big brown eyes.

The little girl cemented a place in Katie's heart right alongside her uncle. She knew exactly what she needed to do.

Later that same evening, Katie sat with her computer on her lap and pecked out her first letter to her mother. She needed to know that Ray was innocent of what she'd accused him.

Dear Mom, let's plan to meet once a month in Seattle. We can go sightseeing and get to know one another as adults. Believe it or not, it took a four-year-old to help me realize that I want to get to know you.

In case you're wondering, Ray is not the man you believe him to be. The woman in the picture is our wedding photographer. She had a special photo printed as a gift for us, and Ray gave her a hug to thank her. I hope this will satisfy your issue with my husband, and you will not interfere again. He is a good man, and he would like to get to know you.

Katie

"It's up to you now, Mom," she whispered and prayed she wouldn't be disappointed.

Ray rang the doorbell at his mother's house.

The door swung open, and she stood there with a raised brow. "This is a surprise. Come in."

"Thanks. We need to talk."

She frowned and led the way to the living room. Mom perched on the edge of her favorite chair and raised her chin.

He sat on the sofa. "I love Katie, and you need to accept that. I'm sorry you met her under bad circumstances, but to be completely honest, our relationship sneaked up on me, or I would have introduced you sooner. We've known each other for a long time but only recently decided to marry."

"Why the rush?"

"Grandfather's will. I had to marry before my twenty-eighth birthday."

She sighed. "I forgot about that silly clause. So is this only a marriage of convenience?"

He shook his head. "No. I'll admit it was at first, but I love her, and so does Emily. I want you to give Katie a chance. I believe if you would, you'd see the qualities in her that I see, and you would grow to love her as I have."

Mom looked down at her folded hands. "Okay. It's difficult to fault the girl, considering she had your best interest at heart."

Relief surged though him, and he shot to his feet. He gave her a hug. "Thank you. You have no idea how much this means to me."

She chuckled and patted his back. "I think I have an

inkling. But how does Katie feel about me? I was…harsh with her."

"I think if you would apologize, that would help."

She nodded. "If I promise to be on my best behavior, will you come for dinner on your birthday?"

He stepped back. "I'll need to check with Katie. I don't know if she has anything planned yet." He hadn't given his birthday much thought. But if Katie didn't want to come, he wouldn't push it. Mom would probably never be her favorite person, but if they could at least get along, he'd be happy.

"Fair enough."

This went so much better than he'd expected. With his plan fully set in motion, he headed to his car where he had a big surprise stashed.

The house looked dark from the outside. Katie held tightly to Emily's hand as they walked along the driveway. Where was Ray? They normally rode home together in the evenings, but when she'd shown up at The Ring, he'd been gone. Concern edged out her irritation that he hadn't at least called to let her know they'd need to ride the bus.

She unlocked the door and pushed into the kitchen. "Hello? Ray, are you here?" Soft music played upstairs. What was going on?

"I'm hungry," Emily said.

Katie's stomach rumbled. "Me, too. How about you go play in your room while I make dinner?"

"Okay." She paused beside the counter. "Can I have a cookie?" She wrapped her arms around her belly. "I'm super hungry."

Katie grinned and went to the fridge. "Wash your hands. Then have a seat at the table. I'll cut up a few apple slices for you. You may have a cookie after dinner." She washed the organic apple, sliced it, then handed it to Emily who frowned.

"I want a cookie."

"I heard. You may have one after dinner."

"I want it now!" She crossed her arms and stomped her foot.

"What's this?" Ray strolled into the room and scooped Emily into his arms. He wore a suit and tie.

"I'm hungry, and Aunt Katie won't let me have a cookie."

"You know what. I have dinner ready for us upstairs."

Katie raised a brow. "You do? What's the occasion?"

He only grinned. "After dinner, Emily is going to spend the night with Grandma and Aunt Hailey."

Katie's gaze shot to his face. "Why?"

He only grinned.

Something was definitely up. Ray looked ready to burst. They'd never eaten upstairs before except for when he brought breakfast or hot chocolate to her room. She followed Ray and Emily as they climbed the stairs.

Ray led them to their niece's bedroom where he had three place settings at the child-sized table. A tray sat on the floor beside it. "Tonight's special is macaroni and cheese. And for the mademoiselle gluten free mac and cheese."

Katie chuckled. "You made two types?"

He nodded and placed the bowls on the table. He pulled out a chair and motioned for Emily to sit, and then he did the same for Katie. He dropped a cloth napkin onto each of their laps.

Emily giggled as only a little girl can. "You're so funny."

Ray waggled his brows, sat, and then offered a blessing for the food. "Eat up."

"You forgot to tell me I needed to catch the bus. We missed the bus and had to wait for the next."

"I'm sorry." His brow furrowed, and the joy faded from his face. "I guess I was a little pre-occupied with planning this evening. I'll do my best not to let that happen again."

She couldn't stay angry. His puppy dog eyes were too adorable. "I forgive you."

"Good. Eat up. I know it's not an amazing meal like you make, but it's the best I could do today."

She took a bite. "It's still hot. How'd you do that?"

"I had it in the warming oven, and I was watching for you. When I saw you coming, I ran it up here. The bowls are hot, so be careful."

"It's yummy!" Emily spooned a bite into her mouth. "Mac and cheese is my favorite." She chewed fast and shoveled bite after bite into her mouth.

Stupefied, Katie didn't know what to do other than

eat. Ray's behavior was way past normal.

The doorbell pealed. Emily sprang from her seat. "I'll get it." She charged from the room before either of them could stop her.

Ray chuckled and stood. "I have her bag packed. You want to grab her favorite blanket and pillow?"

"Sure." Curiosity ate at her. Whatever he had planned must be big since he wanted Emily out of the house for the night. *Oh!* Her eyes widened, and her stomach knotted.

Ray headed for the door and looked over his shoulder. He stopped. "What's wrong? Did the food not settle? You look like you might be sick." He paced toward her and felt her forehead.

"I'm fine. Just very curious about what you're up to."

He ran his hand up and down her arm. "Stop worrying. It's all good. We'd better get downstairs in case that wasn't Hailey at the door."

"Good point." She jetted past him and hustled down the stairs somewhat relieved by his words.

Hailey held Emily. "Hey there." She smiled and put her niece down. "Did she finish eating dinner?"

"I'm done." Emily looked to Katie. "Can we take cookies with us?"

"Sure, if Aunt Hailey says it's okay."

"Of course. I've heard good things about your cookies. In fact, Emily tells me they don't taste funny at all." She wrinkled her nose and made a silly face at her niece.

"That's because they're gluten free."

Hailey nodded. "Let's get going."

Katie handed Hailey Emily's stuff. "Have fun." She crouched low and opened her arms.

Emily flung herself against Katie and squeezed hard. "I love you, Aunt Katie."

"Love you, too. I'll see you tomorrow."

"Okay." Emily hugged Ray then grasped Hailey's hand.

Ray locked up after them then turned to face Katie. "I have a surprise for you."

"I figured. Am I dressed okay?" She took in his suit and worried her bottom lip.

"There's no dress code, but you could change if you'd like."

Well, there was no way she was going to wear the jeans and t-shirt she had on when he wore a suit. "I'll be back in a few minutes." She raced up to her bedroom then yanked open the closet door. She wasn't a clotheshorse, so her options were limited. She wanted to wear a dress, but her only options were the dress she wore to their wedding, or a dainty black sundress. It was a little cool for a sundress, but she could put a shawl over it. She quickly changed, touched up her makeup, then slipped into a pair of kitten heels.

A light knock sounded on her door. "Are you decent?"

"Yes. I'm coming." She opened the door and gasped. "You got me a corsage?" Delicate red and white mini rose buds were nestled in a bed of greenery and baby's breath.

"You look beautiful." He slipped the floral creation onto her wrist then offered his arm. "I hope you'll enjoy this evening."

"Well, you've certainly gotten it off to a great start." She couldn't imagine what he had planned. Especially considering they'd already eaten.

Ray's heart pounded. This was it. His big chance to let Katie know his heart. He led them downstairs, through the kitchen and out the back door.

"Where are we going?"

"To the garage apartment."

She tilted her head to the side. "Okay?"

He grinned at the question in her voice. "Trust me."

"I do."

He saw the truth to her words in her eyes and grinned. "I'm glad." Trust was a big step for her, and he counted himself blessed. He wouldn't break that trust either. He pushed the door open then scooped Katie into his arms.

She squealed. "What are you doing?"

"Carrying you over the threshold. We skipped this the night we were married." He knew she was petite, but having her in his arms like this confirmed it. He placed her beside the door then flicked on the light. Soft music filled the apartment.

Katie gasped. "What did you do?"

He looked around the room and grinned. "It's a

proper wedding reception. I know ours was a disappointment so I tried to create one that you would like, only without the guests. He looked around the space and took in the twinkle lights hanging from the ceiling. Hailey had been a huge help this afternoon when he'd called and explained what he wanted to do.

"You got us a real wedding cake." She waltzed over to the table which held a round, two-tier white wedding cake decorated with edible pearls. "It's so elegant. I love it." She whirled around to face him. Her face glowed in the soft lighting.

He caught his breath. "Me, too. That gluten-free bakery I found put a rush on it for us."

"Why did you do this?" Her voice held only curiosity.

He took a deep breath and let it out slowly. This was it. "I wanted not only to say it but show you that I love you."

"You do?" Surprise lifted her voice.

"Yes. For some time now. But I didn't know how to tell you."

She smiled, staring at him. A serene look covered her face. "I'd say you figured it out. I can't believe you went to so much trouble." She stepped toward him. "I love you, too."

His heart pounded like gloves against a speed bag at The Ring. She loved him. For some crazy reason, he wanted to stop and praise God for setting them up. He was clearly the perfect matchmaker.

Ray opened his arms, and Katie stepped close. He

lowered his head and covered her lips with his. Contentment filled him, and he knew this was exactly where he wanted to spend the rest of his life—with Katie.

Author Note

Dear readers,

Thank you for reading. I hope you enjoyed *The Reluctant Groom*. I've always been a fan of marriage of convenience tropes. I've wanted to write one for years, but since I don't write historical novels I wasn't sure how to pull it off. One night as I was trying to sleep, this story idea came to me. The biggest challenge in plotting this story was making their marriage of convenience acceptable in modern times. I hope I pulled it off.

I enjoy hearing from readers and have several ways we can connect. The links are below. I hope you join my Facebook Readers Group and subscribe to my newsletter. The Amazon link is for you to be notified whenever one of my books releases.

Finally, if you enjoyed this book, please tell a friend. Word of mouth and writing reviews is the best way you can help me continue to do what I do.

Blessings,
Kimberly Rose Johnson

Subscribe to my newsletter at: kimberlyrjohnson.com
Amazon follow: http://amzn.to/2jpZj1C
Facebook: www.facebook.com/KimberlyRoseJohnson

Books by
Kimberly Rose Johnson

Brides of Seattle
The Reluctant Groom

Melodies of Love
A Love Song for Kayla
An Encore for Estelle
A Waltz for Amber

Sunriver Dreams
A Love to Treasure
A Christmas Homecoming
Designing Love

Wildflower B&B Romance Series
Island Refuge
Island Dreams
Island Christmas
Island Hope

Contemporary Inspirational Romance Collection
In Love and War

Contemporary Novella
Brewed with Love